# THE RETIREMENT CURSE

Kim,

Thank You!

Ben Ditsch

# THE RETIREMENT CURSE

B. E. DITSCH

LifeRich Publishing is a registered trademark of
The Reader's Digest Association, Inc.

LifeRich Publishing books may be ordered
through booksellers or by contacting:

LifeRich Publishing
1663 Liberty Drive
Bloomington, IN 47403
www.liferichpublishing.com
1 (888) 238-8637



ISBN: 978-1-4897-0358-3 (e)
ISBN: 978-1-4897-0360-6 (sc)
ISBN: 978-1-4897-0359-0 (hc)

Library of Congress Control Number: 2014921817

Printed in the United States of America.

LifeRich Publishing rev. date: 1/27/2015

This is for you, MOM! You always said I could
do it and now I have. I hope you can read it
from heaven. With much love RIP 9-11-96

# CHAPTER 1

The executive meeting began with the clap of the gavel. The president of the company, sat at the head of the table. He looked around to all his people ...knowing privately he had let them down. They just didn't know it yet! These were people he or his father hired individually. They didn't come from a temporary service, they were friends and family. They were people he loved. People he trusted and people who trusted him. He looked at his right hand man, Bill, a man he has known for forty years, since grade school. He felt almost irritated because most of these people looked ready to retire, and they deserved to retire. Including the "workers" who were retiring. They spent the majority of their lives here, working for him! They didn't know he pilfered so much of the pension money, and how could he tell them. He had to think of a way to get that money back without hurting any of these other executives. So he sat at the head of the table, listening to reports from his constituents, thinking, thinking, and thinking. The head of the budget committee was speaking and, looking around the table, Lenny thought everyone looked tired and bored and especially old! All the heads of departments had a report for each other. They each tried to look interested in other department's reports. Then the head of human resource was giving her speech and talking about all the "workers" who had signed retirement papers. She also asked for a moment of silence for an employee who had recently passed away. As heads were bowed in prayer, the president got his idea. He had to get a hold of as much of this retiree pension money as he could. He had to get it back in the executive pension fund before these guys, who by looking at them, were ready to retire now! He needed to find someone in human resource to do some checking for him. He needed to know how many of the retired workers didn't have family left, how many with no family were taking a lump sum. He needed a numbers cruncher! He didn't even know what all he needed, but he knew he needed a solid plan. First of all, he had to tell Bill and hope he didn't turn him in. They've had other secrets over the years and he never told a soul. He needed him now more than ever. Then he would have at least one person he could talk to about this, it was killing him, not having anyone to talk about it with. After the meeting, he called Bill into his office...

# CHAPTER 2

As she woke that morning, Roselle felt a twinge of guilt. She had gone to the funeral of a friend last night. A friend who had retired a couple months ago... Poor thing only got to enjoy such a short time of retirement. Her friend Carol's family looked like they were in shock. They were all surprised by her death; after all she seemed to be in good health. I guess they should just be grateful she went in her sleep, with no pain. That's how Roselle wanted to pass on to heaven too just wake up to Jesus with all his glory.

When she retires in a couple months she's going to enjoy every second of it. She has been looking forward to retirement for thirty three years! You never know how long it will last! She hoped it would last longer than Carols retirement had lasted. They say if you retire and keep busy, you'll live longer. Roselle knew her grandkids would keep her busy! She was looking forward to at least one week of leisurely reading and napping before their lives took over hers. She knew in her heart that summers would belong to them but they had to go back to school sometime. She was retiring in October this year. That should give her plenty of time to relax before a busy hectic summer with grandkids, she thought with a smile.

Today was going to be a day of shopping and going out to lunch with two of her daughters. They were going to pick her up at ten. She looked at the clock hmm; she had a little while to get ready. As she stepped into the shower she reflected on the life she's had. Divorced parent of three girls with no regrets, although she'll tell you, "The divorce wasn't my idea... I wanted to kill him!! "That thought actually brought a smile to her face. Being the good little catholic girl, she never remarried either. She liked the freedom it allowed her. She could go out with friends, play cards, read a book, and go shopping whatever she wanted with no one telling her she couldn't. Of course she had to take the good with the bad. She had to pump her own gas, pay all her own bills, shovel her own sidewalk, and mow her own grass. Everything that came with owning your own home. Sometimes her son in law would come over and mow but he always mowed her flowers too! She would say something but she enjoyed his company and the flowers did, still bloom. He would just tell her she had too many flowers anyway. She did have a lot of flower beds, and he tried to mow around most of them. Pick your battles she would tell herself.

Her youngest daughter lived close, so she just walked over to her house. As Val walked in the unlocked door she yelled, "Mom, you need to lock your door, I have a key remember? All of us have a key, there's no need to keep it unlocked!" When mom grew up things were safer and no one locked their doors but these are different times she thought to herself. It was really hard to get that through her moms head. Mom yelled "I'll be out in a minute. Is Bobbie here already too?" "No "answered Valerie, "I'm a little early."Standing on the other side of the bathroom door she asked, "Where are we going for lunch? I'm starving, I should've eaten breakfast, but I knew we were going out to lunch. I don't want fast food either! Let's make sure we go to a sit down place. Ok?" Mom answered her, "yes maybe that Mexican place by the mall?"" Ooh yeah I love that place. Let's MAKE Bobbie go there" Val said with a big smile. "Hurry up mom," said Val as she walked to the living room. Val hopped on the stationary bike her mom had in the living room and watched the wrestling tape she had in the VCR while she waited. She usually ran in the mornings but decided she'd see how many calories she was going to have to burn off from lunch. The restaurants gave you way too much food, if you asked her. Bobbie got there before she was ready too. Sitting on her moms bed Bobbie said "Val says we're going to that New Mexican restaurant. That sounds really good. I love their salsa!

Pick up the pace mom, let's get to lunch before the big crowd." "Ok ok I'm ready," said mom. She was thinking, why are we rushing? They don't even open for an hour! They turned the television off, locked the door and left.

The Restaurant wasn't open yet, just like she thought, so they went to the department store nearby for a little bit. Mom liked to shop, even if it meant just looking and not buying anything. Bobbie liked shoe shopping with mom and Val the best because they would take their left shoe off as soon as they entered the department and try on everything in their size! If it fit their left foot and they liked it they would try on the right shoe. They were always sure to put the shoes back on the shelf. Bobbie managed the shoe department at the store she worked at and wouldn't let them be lazy about that. They told her it was job security for someone, but she still made them put the shoes where they belonged. After a half hour of this, the restaurant was open and they walked over to it.

Getting here when they first opened was the best time to get a table. It was a new place and they had free chips and salsa while you waited for your food.

It never failed, every time they were out mom ran into someone she knew. Today it was one of the office cleaners where she worked. Of course she waved to her with a big smile "hello how are you" soon followed. Mom never missed a chance to talk to a friend! Everyone at that office knew mom. She was the highest seniority employee there. She had seen all the comings and goings of the place. She knew who was getting cheated on, who was getting divorced, who was getting married, everything! She also taught all three of her daughters everyone was a human being. Just because someone cleaned the offices instead of working in them doesn't make you a better person. Be kind to everyone. She treated everyone like they were her best friend. They chatted for a while, and then the lady went to be with her own family. The food arrived to the table, as they were finishing their chips and salsa. The three of them were there for an hour and a half eating and talking and laughing. Then more shopping!! When they were finished they went to help mom get her purchases in the house. Bobbie got to the door first and it was unlocked again and she asked Val "didn't we lock this?" "I thought I did, oh well, mom said we must not have locked it right." Val answered her.

After Valerie and Bobbie helped get her things inside, they stayed for just a few minutes. Then, went on their way to their own families. Roselle wouldn't have minded if they brought the grandkids, it was always nice seeing them. She did enjoy her time with just her daughters too. They could talk about grown up stuff. There's plenty of time to take the grandkids with them after she retires she thought with a smile.

# CHAPTER 3

Bill strolled into Lens office casually. He was thinking they were going to discuss the baseball game from this weekend. They had been friends since grade school. Lenny used to get bullied; he wasn't always the bigger of the two of them. Bill would stand up for him then because he had always liked Lènny. He always had the most fun toys. His parents had been good to Bill too. They would take him with them on vacations. He got to go to a lot of places his parents could never have afforded to take him. Skiing in Aspen, Disney world, everywhere they went, they took Bill too. He loved Lenny's family.

He was used to being called into Lenny's office. They usually just talked about sports and life, hardly ever about work. He took one look at his boss and knew something was up though. Bill was shorter than Lenny, and looked up to him figuratively and literally. His boss looked flush, like he was going to tell him something, he didn't want to hear. For a second Bill thought he was going to tell him his dad was sick. When he started talking, Bill was the one who was almost sick.

Lenny asked him to sit down while he shut the door to his office. Bill, I have to tell you something. "I'm not proud of it, but I need your help." At this Bill interrupted him "anything Lenny, you know I'm here for you. We've known each other too long not to help each other out. Do you need an alibi to your wife again?" Bill couldn't understand why Lenny ever cheated on his wife. She was beautiful, blond, very smart, nice ass. Yes, Bill thought about Cindy way too much. "No, no nothing like that" said Lenny. He was secretly thinking, maybe I shouldn't tell him. Is he going to be able to keep this to himself? "Bill, please ... listen to me."He was pleading now and he knew it but Bill didn't have a clue what was coming "This is so hard for me to tell you. I'm just gonna spit it out, no one knows this, I'm trusting you with my darkest secret. I need you to keep this to yourself; I need your help..." In a hushed tone, Bill told him..."I've stolen money from the executive retirement fund. I lost it gambling." Bill gave him a look of unbelievable shock! "I'm so sorry, it just happened! I won money the first time, and was going to put it back and just keep the profit. Then the casino made such a big fuss and treated me like royalty. Hotel comps and women and food. The special treatment was so nice. I had to do it again, they thought I was filthy rich and treated me like I was special, like I was a king. I didn't even want to cheat on Cindy but they were throwing these beautiful women in my face. I didn't want them to think I didn't like gorgeous women. Oh my God, I'm a horrible friend and husband! They pulled me in and got me hooked!"

Bill, after listening quietly, exclaimed through clenched teeth," EMBEZZLEMENT!! Lenny are you freaking kidding me! Holy crap!! You're special alright! You're the president of Coble Communications, for God's sake! I know it's not the biggest company, but we're really starting to grow! There were so many possibilities opening up with cellular communication! "Lenny gave him the shh sign, putting his finger over his lips."Bill, I'm so sorry. I'm working on the gambling, and I only saw those women when I went to the casino. I promise it won't happen again. I told myself I'm never going back there again! "He looked so sincere Bill was inclined to believe him. How could he not help the one man who always believed in him? The man who gave him a job, a good job! The man was his oldest friend. Solemnly he said, "What do you need my help with?"

"First of all, are you with me? You'll help me? You won't tell anyone?" "Tell me what you need Lenny!" After a minute to let it sink in to his friends head, Lenny said "I think we can put the money back in the executive retirement fund from the "workers" retirement fund." "How? It's two separate funds." asked Bill "Lenny said "... Stay with me pal, I kind of have a plan. We have some homework to do though. First of all,

I only took two million dollars. "Through clenched teeth again "ONLY two freaking million dollars!!!" Bill couldn't believe his ears. His friend of it seemed a thousand million years had stolen from him and every executive on this board, he trusted him, hell they all trusted him! Now he wanted him to help him put the money back! He was beside himself with anger but controlled himself because, if he didn't help Lenny, he would never get to retire! He wasn't ready yet, but he had hoped to retire some day!

Lenny started talking about it like it was a math problem. "If each of the "workers" pensions are worth four hundred thousand dollars, on a lump sum payment... Which is what most of them take..."

Bill had to interrupt again; he could almost see the wheels in Lenny's head turning. "Are you seriously talking about stealing it from the "workers" pension fund? We can't just take it from one fund and put it in the other one." Lenny looked at him with a sneer on his lips and answered "not exactly..."

# CHAPTER 4

Roselle was a short woman who had a smile that made everyone feel welcome. She had worked at Coble Communications for thirty three years and if they would have been the kind of company that had a greeter it would've been her. She was just one of those women who were approachable by anyone; she often talked to strangers at the grocery store. She did get a lot of good recipes that way though. I guess you could say she never knew a stranger. She had salt n pepper short curly hair although more salt than she would like to admit. She wasn't as slim as she'd like to be either, but she never was. She had finally decided losing weight was a goal she needed to change. So she opted for being healthy instead, that was hard enough. Being diabetic didn't help either. She was getting better about eating healthy, At least she tried. She had green eyes and a very sharp wit. She liked to think she was totally independent. She rarely asked for help, even when she desperately needed it. When the girls were small, she really could have used some help, but decided to get this job. She took care of her family all by herself. She was a woman of the sixties and her feminist pride kept her from asking for a lot of things. She was a strong woman and radiated happiness. Everyone she met revered her.

Valerie was the youngest of her daughters. She was tall and thin with a more serious outlook on life than her mom, She loved a good joke but rarely laughed at them normally she would just smile and roll her eyes. She was the kind of person who prayed first and asked questions later. She also had green eyes but had a more guarded personality and wasn't as open to strangers talking to her. She thought her mom talked to too many strangers. Valerie was married to Jim, a man with stoic patience, and American Indian in his heritage. You could tell by looking at him, because he had the definitive facial features, and always had his long hair in a braid. He was a big man, six feet tall and broad shoulders. He would help Roselle around the house too, if she asked. They had two sons who by some wild chance were born on the same day of the year, three years apart.

Bobbie was her wild middle child although she settled down a lot after getting married. She had the same green eyes and infectious smile and loved to talk to anyone. She was the only one of her daughters who was short like her and had the curly hair although she wore hers long. She always said that she wouldn't be an old lady till she cut her hair short and wore an apron. She was still a little hippie in some ways. She loved a good joke and would laugh out loud regardless if anyone was close. One of those people whose eyes smiled too. She was always looking for the fun time. She would volunteer at the soup kitchen with her mom just for the quality time they got to spend together. Bobbie loved how everyone at the soup kitchen respected her mom. They would have four huge soup pans ready for mom every Monday.

She made the soup, usually two pans of chicken noodle, a pan of vegetable soup, and a pan of potato or cabbage or whatever the kitchen had in surplus. They would all laugh and tease Roselle about the mess she made while cooking her soup. The people who ate the soup however, loved Mondays because Roselle made the best soup of all their cooks. Bobbie helped unload the bread the stores would donate, and helped set up the serving tables. She got to know a lot of the other volunteers; they all respected and loved her mom. T. J. was her son in law, Bobbie's husband. The same man who would mow her flowers over. He was older than Bobbie and cooled her jets a lot. TJ was a good looking man with dark hair and brown eyes with a twinkle in them. He could be mischievous, but in a good way. He had a big heart and Bobbie loved him. You could tell they were made for each other just by watching them interact together. Roselle would ask him for favors all the time. He was pleasant to be around, and she truly enjoyed his company. He was the one who got them into liking sports, mostly because he never shut up about them. He thought they liked the sports but really, they just liked winning money on the football boards he would be on. You have to have shopping money! They had three children, two sons and a daughter.

Emily was her oldest, the proverbial first born. She looked like her father, Roselle's ex husband. Sometimes that caused problems between the two of them, but they always got through it. They loved each other and it showed. She had his brown eyes and facial features. Emily was tall, bossy, and a natural born leader. She was just starting her own upholstery business and building a house. Always busy, busy, busy. Emily was married to Cam, a fiery Greek man. He had the distinct features of his heritage, the dark hair and dark eyes. He was as tall as Emily; together they could be an intimidating pair. He was one of the head honchos at the factory he worked at. He had worked himself to the top. When he was younger he was the material handler and that's how the two of them met too. The perfect man for Emily, they were both leaders and respected by everyone. The two of them had two daughters.

# CHAPTER 5

They met at the ballpark, a place they were both comfortable. They had played baseball together in high school and college. Lenny was the pitcher and Bill was the catcher. Bill felt like he was still the catcher. Catching Lenny's crap all over again. One of these days he was going to be the pitcher and Lenny could catch his crap! They sat on the bleachers. To anyone passing by, it looked like it was just two old friends having a friendly conversation on a late summer day. But in reality it was a dreaded conversation, at least to one of them. "So, Lenny what's this homework you were talking about?" "Well Bill, we need to find out exactly how many people are retiring soon like within the next two months. Also, how many are opting for the lump sum payment. How many have any dependents under the age of eighteen, or spouses."Bill interrupted "most are divorced women so that might be easier than you think. You're the boss Lenny. You can go in the offices any time you want. I don't want to involve anyone from human resources; they think they know everything about everyone. I've already dated most of them at one time or another." "They do know everything! Isn't there someone we can trust?Asked Lenny ."NOT THAT I KNOW OF... We're going to have to find this information out ourselves! The fewer people involved the better! YOU are going to have to do this homework; you're the one who got us into this mess! You have clearance on the computers, I don't. I'm willing to help you, but I got out of school a long time ago. The homework is on you! This is your baby! You're going to have to know these peoples habits, where they go, what they do in their spare time. All of it!

First of all, Bill went on; make your list of soon to be retirees. Then get back with me." Bill walked away angry, again! He just couldn't believe Lenny did this to all of them. Dirty bastard! He muttered under his breath.

Lenny knew he caused this mess and that Bill was right. He would have to do the homework. He did the crime, now he has to do the time, in research hours. Bill was also right about him being the boss and could get any information he needed on the computer in his office. It was going to be tricky because he didn't want his secretary asking a bunch of questions. He would have to do it when she was on lunch or running errands for him.

That next Monday he asked his secretary, Janet, to go out and buy a present for Cindy, "something expensive, to show his love for her." "It's not her birthday "she replied. She had worked for him so long she knew his whole families birthdays, anniversaries, and even his god children's birthdays. "No, it's a surprise present just because I love her. A man can give his wife a present just because can't he?"

"Yes of course! Are you sure you don't want to pick something out yourself?" She asked. "No, I have some work I need to get started on "he replied. She really didn't mind errands like this. They got her out of the office and it was such a nice sunny day, perfect for shopping. He knew that would give him till at least lunchtime. She liked spending his money. He had sent her out before to get gifts for his family members. She was a good shopper and always picked out the perfect gift.

While she was out, he got busy on his "homework" he figured out that he only needed four perfect candidates. No kids under eighteen still living at home, no spouse, and they had to have opted for the lump sum payout. He figured that would be the easiest money to move to the other pension plan. After all, they had planned on it not being there in the "workers" pension fund, it would've been paid out. The woman who died a couple weeks ago had opted for the monthly payout so all he had to do was transfer that money somehow. It would be trickier but he would do it. Thank God because five people would be too suspicious. Four was going to be hard enough! Holy crap he hadn't even thought about how he was going to carry out his plan! Crap he didn't even have a plan yet! Just four names, one he knew personally, the others he didn't know as well. They had all worked for him for years, but some people were more personable than others. Those he didn't know as well would be first because they would be the easiest. Hopefully none of them had a big dog or a boyfriend he didn't know about. Thank goodness human resources had good files on everyone in the building. Some of the files he couldn't believe what was written and kept track of. One woman was written up for correcting a supervisor's written memo in red ink like a teacher and handing it back to him. How silly he thought. Back to business, he couldn't allow himself to be sidetracked. After all that's what got him into this mess! He now needed to figure out a way to get their pensions without it being suspicious. First he had to learn their habits. Maybe some had allergies, which would be nice, he thought to himself. Maybe some weren't in the best of health, which would be nice too. Gheese he couldn't believe himself. Could he actually pull this off? He was damn well going to try! How hard could it be to kill four little old ladies...?

# CHAPTER 6

Roselle woke up with the sun shining into the living room. Dang it she thought, I fell asleep watching wrestling again! She always meant to go to her bedroom, but living alone, it just really didn't matter. She could fall asleep wherever she wanted! She actually fell asleep on the couch more than she liked to admit. Maybe after she retires, she'll find herself a boyfriend. Then she'll sleep in the bedroom once in a while, she chuckled to herself. She definitely didn't want a husband, but the boyfriend idea wasn't a bad one. The guard at her work would always flirt with her. She liked that; it made her feel like she was still pretty. She thought she might pursue that relationship. Who knows, he could be the love of her life! You never know what life has in store for you. Her daughters thought she didn't get remarried because she was catholic. The real reason was, she didn't want to put up with anyone bossing her. She couldn't stand how some of the girls at work were always saying they couldn't play cards or go shopping because their husband wouldn't let them. "What a crock of shit!" she said aloud to herself.

She went to her kitchen and made a pot of tea. Then

made herself a homemade egg and toast sandwich. She really missed her old dog in the mornings. They had been together for ten years. She was a pit- bull with one blue eye and one brown eye. Her name had been Sara Lee. Roselle would sing the familiar jingle to her and Sara Lee would actually smile. She was a good dog. The only person she would let walk in the house unannounced was Bobbie and they decided it was because the two of their voices were so much alike. She died a couple weeks ago, just lied down in the corner and passed away silently. It was so heartbreaking for Roselle because now, she really was alone. Bobbie and Tj came and lifted her into their truck and took her to the vets so they could cremate her. She had to pick her ashes up later this week. After she retires, she'll get another dog. Right now she needed to mourn and think about what kind she wanted to get. It would probably be another big dog though because she felt safer with a big dog around the house. The little ones were cute but they weren't as good at being guard dogs.

After breakfast she went out on her enclosed patio to read the newspaper. She always read the obituaries, just to make sure she wasn't in them. She could see the neighbor out across the street, and waved to him. Roselle lived in a neighborhood where the houses were close, but being on a corner, she had a nice big private yard. The nosy neighbors on the street out front couldn't see into her house either because it faced the side street. The elderly couple who lived across from her could, but they were so busy taking care of their own issues. They usually just waved from their yard. Which was fine with her. She was the wave at your neighbor kind of person versus the coffee drinking with your neighbor kind of person. She had enough friends from work to keep her busy. Most of her neighbors were elderly, but the young families were starting to move in as people died and or moved in with their kids or just plain retired to another state. It was so nice just sitting on the patio with her tea and paper, in the quiet of the morning. She could hear the birds singing and talking about their night, or whatever birds talk about while they're chirping.

She had to work tonight, but she didn't mind. She was, after all, counting down the days. She had worked all her life, that was the bad thing about being a single parent. You had to pay the bills! She missed a lot of her daughters programs at school and different sporting events. She had to work though; things would be so nice when she didn't have to work anymore. She was only fifty seven years old; the thought of getting to retire so young was comforting. She had a few health problems but nothing she couldn't handle. The diabetes would maybe even get better when she could concentrate on her health more. She would be able to exercise more then too. She fell and broke her ankle a couple years ago and still felt it when it rained. Her ankle would throb with pain on those days. Even that would be better when she could just sit with her feet up. Who knows, with the grandkids getting older she might even move to Florida and get out of Indiana for good! She just couldn't stop smiling. You think about your future when you're young, but for it to finally be here was a whole different story. Everything she had worked so hard for was finally going to pay off. Life was so good sometimes!

# CHAPTER 7

Lenny was in his office, staring into the computer screen. Really though he was thinking about his plan. He needed help from someone besides Bill. He wasn't going to tell him either because Bill didn't want to have anyone else involved. Lenny thought he could get information from other sources though; it WAS his plan after all. They wouldn't even know they were helping him. These women loved to talk. Later this evening he was going to walk through where the workers were. He should be able to find someone he could talk to. Lord knows, everyone liked to "brown nose" the boss! He couldn't walk through that area without being approached by at least a half dozen people. They imagined that he liked them. Some he did like, but the ones who were up his ass as soon as he walked in were the people he didn't like. Always trying to get something from him. He didn't know what they wanted from him; they actually traveled in different circles. None of them were ever at any functions he went to. He did however get invited to their parties at work. Sometimes he would go just for the cake. These women could bake some tasty cakes! Tonight he was going to get something from them...information, stuff he could use in his master plan.

He could see Bills office from his. He had one of the girls from human resources in there. Bill was single and all the girls knew it, they would visit him all day if they could. Lenny couldn't understand why he didn't want to ask any of them any questions. He certainly knew all of them! It would help them out so much! For all he knew Bill was probably sleeping with all of them. He was a player; the girls just swooned around him. He was a good looking guy, not as tall as Lenny or as gray. He was athletic, and all muscle. He could have any lady he wanted, but yet he was still single. He watched as Bill flirted with this girl, the whole time thinking... Ask her, ask her...ask her some of the questions we have!

Put your best face forward Lenny, he thought to himself as he walked in the lunchroom where the women all took their breaks. Hmm homemade cinnamon rolls, must be someone's birthday or something. He helped himself to one of the rolls. Here they come, the brown nosers. "Hi Lenny, what brings you to our neck of the woods? How's your wife? "All sorts of questions."I like your new car. "Anything to make it look like they were actually friends. He chit- chatted with them as he looked around for some of the higher seniority women. They were easy to spot because they all had gray hair and were the loudest group. Their table was marked now too with a cardboard placard. They had been there the longest and were the ones he needed to find out about. It's funny but these ladies didn't kiss up to him at all. They would talk to him but he always had to initiate the conversation. There were four of them sitting at a table together. "Hello ladies," he said, as he sat down with them. They all had a roll except one. "No cinnamon roll Mary?" "No I can't have them" she said. "Cinnamon makes my throat swell up and I didn't bring my allergy pen with me." "That's too bad" said Lenny "they look really good," as he took a bite. The other women reminded Mary to start carrying her allergy pen with her. You never know when you're going to need it they said. Mary just nodded her head and said "ok, ok". Lenny made a mental note, Mary-allergic to cinnamon. As he's sitting, eating with them, Roselle walks in, he notices that everyone in the room talks to her. It's like she floats from table to table, everyone calls her over. He also notes, she didn't get a roll either. "No roll for you Rosie?" "No, I'm trying to quit "she answered, with a smile. He talked to them a little longer then left because they weren't giving him any information he didn't already know. That group was a tough crowd! They were never impressed with any of the name dropping he did. They were their own little clique. They talked to the lower seniority but they confided in each other. He did like Roselle though; she had her own spunk and was a very smart lady. It was her who was written up for correcting a supervisor's memo and handing it back to them. What a hoot! Yes, Roselle was going to be the toughest one on his list. Everyone would miss her, including Lenny. That reminded him he should talk to his supervisors too. They knew what was going on with the women, or at least they should! He encouraged his supervisors to get to know the workers, we spend a lot of time together, might as well get to know each other. It made for more of a family like atmosphere. If someone was going through a rough patch at home, it can affect their work time too. We have to help each other out, like a family should

# CHAPTER 8

Roselle answered her phone; it was Emily, her oldest daughter. She rarely stopped by but always remembered to call. She was so busy with their new house in Osceola and her business. Today they were talking about after she retires. Emily was trying to talk her into going on one of those singles cruises. "Ha! I get seasick and can't swim. I'm going to have to meet someone a different way "she told her. Emily just wanted her to get out more and not be one of those people who sit around bored doing nothing. "Don't worry; I have a lot of things on my list. I've been planning this for thirty years, I'll be busy!" Then Emily decided to tell her all the updates on the new house, to change the subject, after listening for about five minutes, Roselle told her "she had things to do before she got ready for work tonight." They said their goodbyes. Sometimes it just irked her that her own kids didn't think she could do anything without them telling her. My goodness, I thought I was done with them knowing everything when they got out of their teens, I guess not, she thought. I'm only fifty seven but they acted like she was seventy or something. I'm still young enough to plan my retirement ... Gheese! Wait till they get my age, then they'll know how ridiculous they were being! She got up and stretched, looked at the stationary bike in the living room. Her daughters put it in there so it might tempt her to get on it. She knew she should get her butt on that bike. She also knew she was so close to retiring that it could and would wait just a little longer. Ugh she knew the day was coming when she would have to get serious about exercise. You would think you get to a certain age and it doesn't matter, but it still does. Your inner self still felt like a teenager while your outer self said, whoa we are not doing that again! It was sad to realize that some things were going to be in your past from now on. Getting up from the floor is definitely not the same in your fifties. She couldn't think of anything physical that was easier as you get older. "Healthy not skinny "she repeated to herself, as she walked into the kitchen. After she cleaned the kitchen from breakfast and lunch she got ready for work. It was nice working in an office that had a casual dress code. You did still have the younger girls who would get way too dressed up. Trying to catch a supervisor's eye or Bill the Vice President who strolled through once In a while. Bill was a good looking guy and they all enjoyed looking at him, but the older seniority knew he had dated half the women in the front office and was a player in every sense of the word. The same ones were up the head honchos butt when he walked through too, but he was married and loved his wife. If they only knew, his wife was one of the sweetest people you would ever meet. She had met her at one of the volunteerism award luncheons, sweet as pie and beautiful. That didn't stop them from trying though. Her group of friends always called these girls the gold diggers because that's what they were after.

She stopped at Bobbie and Tj's house in South Bend on the way to work. They lived in a neighborhood outside of town called River Park. They always ate healthy and Bobbie would make enough supper, for her to take some to work. Yum meatloaf, that's something that's hard to make for one person unless you want to eat it for a week. She really appreciated the healthy suppers. It helped keep her diabetes in check. She only had time to pick up her supper and go because she wanted to get to work early. When she got to work, she went to her locker, then to the lunchroom. She had to smile because someone had made a cardboard nameplate that read "retiree table" and put it on her friends and hers table. There were a lot of them retiring within the next month or so. Everyone was telling her congratulations, she knew they were just glad to move up a spot on the seniority list. That's okay though, that's how she felt thirty three years ago. When she got to her friends she saw Lenny was there. She thought to herself, he must have smelled those cinnamon rolls all the way in his office. He liked his sweets! He asked her "why she didn't get one," she told him "she was trying to quit." Really it was because of her diabetes but that's none of his business! He called her Rosie too, she hated that! Her family and friends were the only ones she let call her Rosie and as much as she really did like and respect him, he was neither! After he left, she asked her friend Mary, "why was he here?" She answered "we think he wanted a cinnamon roll, you know how he likes his sweets! Haha" After she talked for a little bit, she went in the offices to her computer table and got busy. She looked around to see what supervisor they had tonight. Oh great the idiot one that can't spell. In her head she called him "dumb Derek." He wrote her up before. He just couldn't stand that

Roselle knew more about the English language than he did. He was always bragging about being a college graduate. It didn't help that she would correct his memos with red ink and hand them back to him! She was just trying to help! Either way she better put her nose to the grindstone and get to work. She didn't want to get in trouble right before she retires, or did she? I guess that all depended on if he sent out another memo. She smiled and waved to her friends Joan and Marge and got to work.

# CHAPTER 9

Lenny went back to his office. Those women could really make the sweet stuff! He loved that just about every night, with so many retiring, there was something sweet in the lunchroom. He never even asked, he would just help himself. No one had the balls to tell him he couldn't have any. He truly felt it would probably hurt their feelings if he didn't go in and get a piece of whatever was there. Good timing he thought too. Now was when he needed to spend as much time as he could around the workers. It wouldn't hurt if Bill strolled through more often too. The younger seniority women usually swarmed around him though. They might think it was odd if he spent too much time around the older gals. He could always say he was going to miss them and wanted to sit with them awhile. Plus the added cakes and rolls were nice but Bill didn't eat sweets too much. He tried to stay on a healthy regimen of food and exercise. That's probably why he looked so athletic. I guess Lenny was a little jealous of him. Bill was single and could play the field where Lenny had met the love of his life and married her. Who was he kidding, he'd cheated on the" love of his life" he disgusted himself. He loved her so much and didn't know what he would do if she left him. His secretary, Janet, had bought her a beautiful necklace for him. When he gave it to her, she just looked a little confused. "What's this for?" He'd told her it was "because he loved her so much and wanted her to have it."She had him put it on her and marveled at how sparkly it was. He kissed her and they made the most passionate love they had ever had. He didn't know she just read an article in one of her magazines about unexpected gifts signal something's going on.

Cindy got up the next morning, looked at her necklace and wondered... Was something up or was it because he really did love her??? He had gotten her presents in the past that weren't for her birthday or anniversary. She was going to enjoy this but try to keep an eye on things. Magazines weren't always right! Every woman needed some sparkle in her life!

Back to the moment, Lenny turned his computer on. Janet had already left for the day. She was a feisty red head who knew more about him than she probably should. Cindy liked her though, and that was a good thing. He learned a long time ago, happy wife – happy life. He liked Janet too. She knew her job and did it well. He could ask her to do all this "homework" but didn't want to get her involved. He already suspected she knew about the women or at least a woman. She hadn't asked too many questions when he asked her to shop for him. That can only mean... She already knows or suspects something. You just can't trust a woman's intuition! As long as she doesn't get wind of the plans he has going on now. He was fine; she could think whatever she wants.

He pulled Mary's name up so he could read her complete file. Wow, she had so many allergies, they were on her file. Ahh she's allergic to dogs too. That was nice. At least he knew he wasn't going to get bit. Then he thought of another plan... He needed to talk to one of the supervisors.

He went out on the office floor, looked around and didn't see any supervisors. So back to the lunchroom, there they were. There were three supervisors scheduled at all times. They weren't supposed to take break together. As soon as they saw him, they tried to look like they were having some kind of meeting. Sure, three cinnamon rolls on the table; he knew this was a meeting of the stomachs! He hated liars, ha! He was the biggest one of them all! Because of that he decided to ignore protocol and sat down with them. They were a little nervous until he said, "gentlemen, nobody in here but you guys? How often does that happen? "They all in unison said "never! We just saw the rolls and you know these women can bake!" "Yes I know "Lenny said, patting his stomach. He saw the cleaning lady come in just then. She got right to work, with three supervisors and the head honcho watching her. At that the supervisors all feigned work and got up and left. They had eaten their rolls while Lenny was talking to them. Lenny talked to the cleaning lady for awhile and noticed the whole time he was in there none of the women came in for a break.

That gave him an idea...

# CHAPTER 10

Roselle had an uneventful night except those dang cinnamon rolls! They smelled so good but she didn't have one. She ate her meatloaf and half a sweet potato and green beans. Bobbie used her old meatloaf recipe with a few healthy tweaks. She used oatmeal instead of crackers, and added chopped spinach too. Overall it was delicious. Her friends were a little jealous because they couldn't just stop at one of their kid's house and get a nice plate of supper. Bobbie had her favorite grand dog too. His name was grunt and he was a lab collie mix. He would wag his whole butt when he saw her pull up in front of their house. She would go in and sit on the recliner and before she knew it, grunt was on her lap, and he was NOT a lap dog! She kept peanut butter bones in her pocket just for him. She just loved him. He was a good egg!

She drove home alone as usual. She always kept a hat on the headrest of the passenger seat, so it looked like two people were in the car. Her friends thought it was a crazy idea. She had read about it in some magazine. It worked; she always made it home safe. It was a nice late summer night. The stars were out. She had named the two brightest ones after her brothers who had passed away. One in the Vietnam War and the other from Cancer. She still had a sister and two brothers alive but they lived in Ohio and Texas. Her sister, Elizabeth, is who Bobbie named her daughter after. They called her Liddy and her sister's nickname was Dolly. Both were family nicknames though and they did have the same first names. It's nice to pass tradition down through generations. Bobbie's boys were named Michael and Joshua, biblical names. Who would have ever thought Bobbie would name her kids after people in the bible? She raised so much hell during her teen years. All of her grandkids were at least fifteen except Val's boys, Marty and Dale, They were getting there though. Emily's two girls, Roselle who was named after her, and Mallory were the same ages as Bobbie's kids. That's why she didn't mind them shopping with them. They were more manageable now. Lunch was a different story! They ate like they were starving all the time, even the girls. I guess she should be glad they didn't have any eating disorders like so many girls these days were having. None of them were overweight either; they all stayed busy with athletics. She only took them out to lunch a couple at a time. That made it affordable and they could go to nicer restaurants.

She arrived home safe and sound like she knew she would. Being late in the evening, the old couples across the street were up getting some kind of snack or something. The old man looked out the kitchen window and Roselle waved to him. Sometimes she wondered if he was waiting for her to get home. It was like he was watching out for her and she was okay with that. Good neighbors are hard to find. It's not that he could do anything except call police but at least he watched for her. It made her feel safer knowing he was there, and watching. She never noticed if he stayed up late on her days off from work though, probably not. Knowing him, he would watch for when her car was gone in the evenings and knew which nights to stay up for her.

There was that stationary bike staring her in the face. After she changed clothes she hopped on. She figured she could ride it for at least twenty minutes. Nope she was wrong; ten was all she could muster. I guess that's better than none. She decided she could ride for ten minutes as fast as she could, that would be good enough for now. She had plenty of time to ride it after she retired. She made a mental note to ride it for ten minutes minimum a day till she retired. After that all hell was going to break loose.

She really missed Sara Lee now. It seemed like she talked to herself more, where before at least she was talking to the dog. Somehow that made it better. She was getting another dog as soon as she retired and has the time to put in for a new dog. She didn't want a puppy though, that's way too much work! It was her retirement time, not time to chase after a puppy and clean up poop!

# CHAPTER 11

Lenny called Bill and asked "if he could get a hold of a couple syringes." His dad was diabetic so he knew he could. That's probably why Bill took such good care of himself. He never really thought about it before now. While he waited, he boiled some celery down and mashed it. Then puréed it some more then drained the juice. Now it was injectable. He kept it in a small vial. Cindy had gone with her sister, to visit their parents a few towns away. So he had the house to himself. He made chicken noodle soup too since the house smelled like celery. "Gotta cover your tracks dude" he told himself.

Bill brought the syringes over. His dad would never miss them. He ordered them by the case because it was cheaper. He wasn't sure what Lenny was going to do with them, but he was sure it was part of the plan. He still couldn't get over what Lenny had done. He was positive he wasn't going down for him though. This was his mistake not Bills! The house smelled like chicken noodle soup. He kind of chuckled as he asked Lenny. "Are you the cook around here? I always thought Cindy did the cooking." Lenny answered him, "just for today. Cindy went to her parents with her sister. "They talked about baseball and Bill thought maybe Lenny had given up on this idea and was going to work harder to put the money back legally.

It was Sunday but Lenny knew Mary worked tonight. He also knew there were times the lunchroom was empty. With the allergies she had he was sure she brought her own lunch. Everyone marked their lunches with their names like territory. This shouldn't be too hard; his only hope was she had soup or something he could put the celery juice into easily. She had so many allergies he actually felt he was doing her a favor! She couldn't have enjoyed the food she ate; it had to be so bland. Celery was on her list but it was so flavor less she would never know!

He went to the offices on the weekends a lot. They were a twenty four - seven kind of company. No one ever questioned why he was there. It was his company; he could do what he wants.

He snuck into the lunchroom when he knew everyone was working, from his earlier observations. Including the supervisors! He opened the fridge looked for Mary's name on a lunch. Holy crap doesn't anyone on nights eat out of the machines! It was full of lunch boxes! He finally found it, BINGO she had a thermos, and it had to be soup because they had free coffee and tea in the lunchroom. He opened it and wanted to yell whooohoo, but he poured the celery juice in and replaced the lid. He was amazed he didn't even have to use the syringe. He got the hell out of there, and went to his own office.

He began to get totally engrossed in his own work. Reports from every satellite office plus his own departments. They were mundane, but somebody had to read them and he was that somebody. His father had started this company and now it was his by default. He really didn't mind, it was a good living. It was really starting to expand with everyone wanting cellular phones now. An idea he thought was insane. A couple hours later as he was still reading reports, he could hear people screaming and yelling. He ran to the lunchroom to see what the commotion was. Oh my god someone yelled call 911! Call 911! Somebody else yelled check her purse for her allergy pen! Most of the high seniority people were in there. Freaking out and in shock. Mary's face and throat kept getting bigger and bigger. Her face was turning blue oh my God it was a sight none of them would forget in a long time! Roselle was holding her hand trying to soothe her. There was no soothing her though and she couldn't feel a pulse in her wrist anymore. Mouth to mouth wouldn't help because no air was going in or out. Her throat was closing. Everyone was watching, waiting, hoping Roselle could bring her back, like her smile was magic or something. She wasn't smiling though. Roselle gave in to just praying. They were both on the floor. Everyone was frantic! Mary had had reactions before at work, not as bad as this though. Joan was going through her purse, nothing! No one had an allergy pen! The women and Lenny all had a look of horror on their faces. The ambulance finally arrived but they were too late. They called the coroner who came and pronounced her dead, and took her to the morgue. It was a sad night at Coble communications. The women were walking around like they were zombies or something. Everyone had been horrified from the scene at lunch.

# CHAPTER 12

Bill went straight to Lenny's office as soon as he got there. "I heard what happened last night" he said. Lenny told him "yes, I was here, it was awful!" He wasn't going to tell Bill that it was part of the plan. But Bill was giving him a sideways look, like he was asking. Lenny ignored it. He told Bill "we're going to have to talk to the women today about last night. There was a lot of high seniority here. You would think they'd want to work days."" I know, to each his own" said Bill. He didn't concern himself with what hour's people liked to work. The high seniority pretty much picked their own hours and as long as they showed up, it didn't concern him. He thought it was nice that they let the women who had school-aged kids work days.

They went into the big office where the workers were, together. They gave the women their condolences and said they had already ordered flowers from corporate and were sending several meat trays for after the funeral. The women just nodded, they were all in shock and none of these women were even there to see the horror. Lenny wasn't sure he would ever get Mary's face out of his mind. It really was horrible!

He thought she would just die. He didn't know about the blueness, and the swelling, it really was the worst death he'd ever seen in person.

As they walked back to their own offices, he told Bill, "that's two, because the woman who died a couple months after retiring had taken the monthly payout, so they had that money too. "He had already transferred her money into the executive pension fund. It was nice having someone he could talk to about all of this, even if he wasn't telling him everything. He wasn't sure he would ever admit to this one. Lenny was actually thinking, so far it's been easy except for the guilt he had in his stomach. He threw up last night in his private bathroom after the ambulance left. To know that he had caused that horrific scene sickened and excited him.

He knew he was going to have to wait a couple weeks till the next one. The first one was so easy; he couldn't believe he did it! He couldn't believe it excited him so much too. What was he turning into? He did still have to hope the morgue didn't catch it. He was hoping they would say it was unfortunately an anaphylactic reaction that caused her death. She was allergic to so many things. He himself couldn't believe she didn't have an epinephrine pen with her. She did pack her own lunch and was disciplined enough not to eat anything she didn't bring with her. He wasn't going to celebrate till he heard the coroner's determination. Next time though, he didn't want to be anywhere close when it actually happened. Once was enough for him.

Bill couldn't believe he was even thinking about the plan after such a horrible death happened right in front of him. It seemed like his friend had become heartless and uncaring. How callous of him to say... That's two! What the hell was wrong with him, he thought. He wasn't really sure if it just happened or if Lenny caused it to happen. Either way he needed to be careful, what would stop Lenny from killing him? He didn't trust him anymore!

They still had to give the same speech to the night crew. That would be the hard one because most of these women were here last night and witnessed it. How horrible!!!

Roselle, Joan, and Janice were all sitting together that night when Lenny and Bill walked over to their table in the lunchroom. They looked a little green, Bill thought. Lenny started with condolences and told them about the flowers and food the company had ordered. Roselle was the first to say anything." I can't believe she didn't have an allergy pen with her; she's allergic to dang near everything!

She was getting so thin, and could hardly eat anything with flavor anymore. It's just sad, sad, sad! Poor thing and they can't even have the funeral right away because her kids live out of state. "They also all agreed that if they do an autopsy, it's just going to show it was her allergies.

When they started talking about her kids and what a jerk Mary's ex husband was, Lenny and Bill made their exit.

The women were saying how sad it was that she never got to retire! Signed her papers but never got to enjoy it. They all shook their heads, such a shame. Poor Mary...

# CHAPTER 13

All the women in the office were in shock still. The younger seniority who were working that night looked at Roselle and Joan with more respect than they ever had shown them before. They always liked them but the older ladies pretty much stayed to themselves. They all felt bad for Mary's family.

What a horrible way to die, and right before she retired. Roselle and Joan were talking and they still could not get over Mary not having an allergy pen with her. Joan said, "If I was that allergic to everything I'd have that pen on a necklace." Roselle agreed, and then thought out loud... "Maybe Mary had given up. She used to have that pen in her purse all the time, but the more she was allergic to things the less she had it on her. Remember a couple days before she died, she didn't have a cinnamon roll because she didn't have it." "She was getting paper thin too "Joan said."Yes, yes she was and her kids being out of state. She did seem sad lately didn't she? Her eyes were sad."Joan agreed with Roselle. The two of them had decided Mary had given up on her own life. They felt Mary must have stopped carrying her pen so that if she did have a reaction, it would kill her. "I'm sure she didn't think it would turn out like that and be so horrifying for everyone around her. At least she was at peace and, in heaven she could eat whatever she damn well wanted! Mary's family wasn't even going to have a funeral. They were going to have her cremated and just have a memorial service at her church" said Roselle How sad they thought. This woman raised her kids by herself just like Roselle. That was all the thanks they could give her. The two of them decided it really wasn't any of their business; maybe her kids didn't have a lot of money. Lord knows their own kids weren't rich either. The kids would get her life insurance but not her pension. So sad because she worked so hard all her life. Roselle declared that "she didn't want to die on a day she had to work! If she was going to die it would at least be on her day off!" Joan agreed! They walked into the office together from the lunchroom.

Lenny was there that evening too. He knew he had to at least wait a week before the next one. He was still waiting on the coroner's report from Mary. He was optimistic though. She had severe allergies and no epinephrine pen. Why, he didn't know. He was glad though because that made it so easy. He knew he had taken a chance that she would have her pen with her, but she didn't have it the other day and he had hoped she still didn't. It was like God was helping him or Satan, was more like it.

Mary's children had asked if they could come up and clean out their mom's locker. Lenny had to give them a specific time because the building had a keypad code to get in. Someone would have to be at the door to let them in. That was part of the problem with the night she died. The ambulance crew couldn't get in because the guard wasn't there to let them in. No one knew Lenny had sent him on a wild goose chase on the seventh floor after pulling a fire alarm on his way to the lunchroom. He had never in his life been this devious. It was working for him though and he knew he was enjoying it way more than he should!

He decided that he would go with the guard to let Mary's kids in. They all lived out of state and according to the ladies, weren't involved with their mom as much as they should have been. It was just her oldest daughter; she asked "if anyone had the combination to the lock on her mom's locker." Lenny just had the guard cut it off. No one was going to need it now he thought. As soon as she opened it she started crying, right there on the shelf was an allergy pen. If only someone would have known her moms combination. "Damn! Why was she always so private! It cost her, her life!" Lenny gave her daughter a big bear hug and told her how sorry he was. She didn't know how much he really meant it. He asked her "have you gotten the report from the coroner yet." "Yes I have it right here" as she pulled it out of her purse. "I didn't know if I needed to prove I was her daughter to get her things. They don't have the death certificates copied for me yet. The coroner ruled it death by Anaphylaxis shock. We all knew mom had allergies but she never told us how bad they were getting. I just talked to her two weeks ago ..." With tears in her eyes, "she never said anything. I noticed she was so thin too, when I went to the morgue and gave permission to release her body to the crematorium, it breaks my heart."

All of the women gave her their condolences. They even let Roselle and Joan and some of the other high seniority women leave their stations so they could come out and talk to her.

When she was ready to leave Lenny and the guard helped her take her moms things to her car. She had books and extra shoes and sweaters, and all kinds of things in her locker. Thirty years of work life stuffed into two boxes. How sad.

Lenny was ecstatic! He had to keep himself from smiling, at least till he was completely alone...

# CHAPTER 14

Lenny went back to his office after helping Mary's daughter carry her things to her car. He couldn't contain himself and let out a big silent Whooohoo after closing his door. Yes! He had gotten away with it. WOW he couldn't believe his luck. Bill didn't have a clue either. He tried to get Lenny to tell him if he did it or not. He just acted like he was as mortified as everyone else. Part of him actually was too. When did he get so devious and murderous! Has this been inside him all his life? He sure could have used it in grade school when he was getting bullied.

Now he had to figure out how he was going to get his next target. He knew who it was going to be, Janice, but he didn't get a lot from her file. She never was written up. It didn't say if she was diabetic or anything. No allergies, damn, because that was just too easy. It sure would have been nice to have another easy one. He decided to scope out her house. She worked the overnight shift, but he was sure she still had one son living at home. He was nineteen though and not a threat to her pension money. He hadn't planned on any of them having kids at home but she was in pretty bad shape he thought, and would be an easy target. Her son was a senior in high school and Lenny knew that meant he was most likely never home. He was going to have to get crafty with this one. Her son played football, and it was late summer. School hadn't started yet, but when he played in high school they had lots of practices this time of year. They liked to call them two-a-days. He hated them when he played! They worked you till you were bone tired. Then told them all to go home and go to bed! The coaches thought it would keep them away from their girlfriends. He had met Cindy in high school and nothing stopped him from seeing her. Hopefully her son was as tired as he always was, but didn't have a girlfriend. What was he thinking; it would be better if he did have a girlfriend. Most of the guys on his team didn't though, so he was just going to have to wait and see. He needed to get inside her house, see if she had any medication she might accidentally overdose on. She might have a hobby that could be deadly. Whatever, the bottom line was, he needed to get inside her house! He decided he wasn't going to involve Bill unless he absolutely had to. He was acting kind of strange around Lenny. Like he could see horns in his head that no one else could see. Great! He thought to himself, now I'm getting paranoid!

He checked the schedule, Janice had to work Thursday and Friday. He was going to have to wait. It's only a couple days away. He could handle it. That would give him time to go by her house and see when her son was at practice. He could tell by her address which high school he would go to. He actually was hoping her son was a kicker, and then he wouldn't be big like a defensive tackle. Lenny was big but he knew he wasn't eighteen anymore either. He didn't think he could take on a high school senior, plus if her kid caught him... He would have to kill him too! Now he wished he would have worked out with Bill whenever he had asked him. If the kid was huge, he decided he would have to ask Bill for help.

Janice was in worse shape than him, that might come in handy too he thought.

He memorized her address and drove past her house on his way home. No one was outside, no big teenage boys. He figured her son was probably at football practice. The neighbor's houses were pretty close too. He didn't hear any dogs though, but he was driving by not walking. He saw there was an abandoned building across the side street. He could use that for parking when he did decide to sneak in. There were cars in the parking lot now. The neighbors probably use it to keep their cars off the street. They probably all have teenage drivers, and that means extra cars. It also meant, they were used to strange cars in that lot. Kids had so many friends.

Lenny went home and spent the evening with Cindy. They went out to dinner, then went home and watched television. Boring... He thought to himself but he knew he was never going to that casino again. A boring night is what his mind needed anyway. This conniving and planning was taking a toll on him. He noticed his hair was even getting grayer. Cindy liked cuddling with him in front of the television anyway. She truly was the love of his life. He hoped he never had to tell her what he was doing. He kind of felt, he was doing it for her too. It was their future he was worried about. Who was he kidding...? He knew it was to save his own sorry ass from going to prison for embezzlement! So, murder people instead! He hadn't got caught, so in his mind, that made it all right. He was pathetic! His own conscience wouldn't even shut up and let him have a peaceful night with his wife!

# CHAPTER 15

Bobbie heard about Mary through the grapevine. She called her mom and asked if she wanted to go out to breakfast. She knew if anyone knew the whole story it would be her mom! Roselle didn't usually go out to breakfast because she didn't like to eat alone, especially in public. At home it was no big deal. She asked Bobbie where she wanted to meet. "How about that place by the shopping center?" "Sounds good to me" said Roselle," I'll meet you there in half an hour."

They met for breakfast, just the two of them. Emily and Val were at work and all the kids were in school. The husbands were all at work too. Bobbie loved breakfast; it helped her with her diet because she would be too full to overeat at lunch or supper. She ordered her favorite, Mexican skillet. Roselle ordered eggs and ham and toast. Potatoes came automatically. It was a nice cozy restaurant with booths for privacy.

"So tell me what happened at work a couple days ago!"Said Bobbie, she was ready to hear the whole story and not bits and pieces that she had already heard. Roselle told her" I don't know if I even want to think about it till after

I eat. It was horrible!" "I know" Bobbie answered," I bet it was. Oh my god, how are spirits at the office?" Roselle told her "they were pretty down, but it was getting better. Mary is in a better place. She had gotten to where all she could eat was soup anymore. She was so thin too. She couldn't turn sideways because you would lose sight of her. It was awful! At least in heaven she can eat whatever she wants." Roselle told Bobbie "the saddest part to me was when her daughter came to clean out her locker. All her things fit into two boxes. Thirty years of work, in two boxes. You would think that thirty years of work would have to be carried out on a flat cart at least! When her daughter opened her locker there was an allergy pen right on the shelf too." "What!"Bobbie said in disbelief. "Joan and I think she gave up," said Roselle "She was probably hungry" Bobbie said. "I just feel so bad for her "Roselle said."Her kids all lived out of state and she didn't get to enjoy her grandkids. I guess you never really know how good you have it till you see someone else's life." "Yeah that's true" said Bobbie."Most people only think about their own lives, that's all they have to go by. You see other people but unless they tell you what's going on in their lives, you don't know. So you figure their lives are like your own. Most people don't like to admit that they're lonely." Roselle said "yeah I guess. It's just sad that Mary was so lonely even in a room full of people. She never truly opened up to anyone. She would smile and have fun with the rest of us, but never expressed her own feelings. "That's too bad" Bobbie said "maybe you ladies could have helped her." "Well we knew her ex husband was an ass hole" said Roselle "Ha! Aren't they all, according to you ladies "Bobbie teased."Of course they are! "Roselle said, and they both laughed at that. While they were having a cup of tea after they ate, Roselle told Bobbie all the gory details. Enough that Bobbie hoped her, or actually anyone she knew, would never have any allergies. The whole scene sounded absolutely horrid! If she would've been there she probably would have nightmares every night for a while.

They then packaged up the leftovers in to go boxes and got up to leave. Bobbie was surprised that they didn't run into anyone her mom knew. I guess there's a first time for everything she thought. Roselle paid for their breakfast and they walked out to the parking lot. When they parted Roselle told Bobbie to "carry on." That was her signature good bye. "Love you mom thanks for breakfast" said Bobbie.

# CHAPTER 16

It was finally Thursday, Lenny felt like he had been waiting for a month. Tonight he was going to case Janice's house. He figured if he went around two in the morning, her son would be asleep. By then the football tiredness would sink in whether he had a girlfriend or not. What he didn't figure in was Cindy. Crap what could he tell her? He thought maybe he could slip a sleeping pill to her somehow. Great! Now I'm drugging my wife! He couldn't believe his own behavior. He knew then that he needed to get this all done, the quicker the better! He had to keep in mind a certain timeline though. He couldn't have four women plus the one who really did die from natural causes happen so close. He was pushing it with one every two weeks. The women in the offices would just get over one death and another one would happen.

That day he went in to work around ten. He was the boss; they never knew what time he would be in the office. Janet, his secretary was used to it. She knew he had some days that he didn't come in at all. He went in at night a lot too. He liked knowing all his people, day shift, night shift, and even the swing shift people. They all knew him too. That's the way his dad ran the company and he taught Lenny the value of knowing your people. He made it his business to know everyone's names. He had slacked a little lately and didn't know a few of the new hires names. He would get to it though.

Bill came into his office, "what's new Lenny? I think the women are getting over Mary's death." "Yeah I think so too, I noticed the "retiree table" in the lunchroom was laughing again." Said Lenny "Yeah they're a funny bunch" said Bill."So what do you have going on this weekend?" Bill asked. He whispered, "did you decide to put that money back a different way, a legal way?" Lenny ignored that question and told him, "Cindy and I are going to the beach house for the weekend." He had already promised her. They bought this beach house a couple years ago and Cindy loved going to it. He might even take tomorrow off and go a day early. Cindy would love that!

Lenny had been so busy this past month he hadn't been there at all. It was going to be a nice peaceful weekend on the beach, he needed that. "Bill, you and whoever you're dating this week are welcome to come up. You can stay in the guest room. "Bill told him, "we just might!" It was supposed to be really warm this weekend and what woman didn't like going to the beach! "I'll bring some steaks for the grill Saturday night." "That sounds great, "Lenny said. "We'll see you then."

Bill went back to his office to try and decide which woman he was going to ask. He knew he could take any woman he wanted. He was dating three women right now. This was going to be a tough decision. Some just start to get possessive after a weekend trip with a man though, and he wanted to avoid that! He liked playing the field. They all knew about each other, he was always honest about that on the first date.

The day went on with nothing unusual happening. Lenny did his usual stuff, including checking the lunchroom for cake or cookies. He really was just biding his time till he could leave and go home. Roselle and Joan and Marge called him over to their table. "We heard about the coroner's report, and didn't want you to feel bad about it. There wasn't anything anyone could do, "they said. Except maybe not put the allergen in her soup Lenny thought to himself. "We remember when your dad still worked here. How is he doing in his retirement? "Lenny told them "his dad was doing wonderful, and often asked about the business." They asked him to tell his dad hello for them. Lenny told them he would. Knowing full well he wasn't telling his dad anything about anyone from work. His dad never asked him about work. When he retired he retired for good. He really didn't care what happened at work anymore; he had his pension and was living his life the way he always wanted to live.

Lenny went home at seven and had supper with Cindy; they talked about the upcoming weekend at the beach. He started acting tired around midnight, actually he was tired but his day wasn't finished yet. He had slipped a sleeping pill in Cindy's last glass of wine; she should be passing out pretty soon. They went upstairs to their bedroom. He put pajamas on knowing she would be asleep any time now. BAM she was out! That stuff worked better than he thought. It was just an over the counter pill he picked up from the drug store. Combined with all the wine she drank, it did its job. Life's little miracles he thought. He slipped back into his clothes and left quietly.

He got to Janice's neighborhood a little earlier than he'd planned. One o'clock in the morning, the whole area was asleep. There weren't any dogs barking either, even they were asleep. Wow! He tried the back door and it was unlocked. What's up with people who don't lock their houses at night! He should probably have a safety talk with these women. No neighborhood is that safe! He was glad though. No dog either...yay! He noticed the hallway light was on upstairs, and headed that way quietly. He found her son's bedroom; the kid was out cold, drooling on his pillow case. He knew how tired the kid was... Been there done that! Lenny closed his door so he wouldn't accidentally wake him. He went to Janice's room and was looking in her master bathroom medicine cabinet. Hmm oxycodone, she must have had something happen lately because it was a new prescription. Too much of that can kill you, but he didn't know how he could force an overdose with her son right there. Although her son hadn't woke up yet, and he had made some noise. It seemed like every squeak of the steps would wake him, but nothing! He was a big boy too, probably a defensive tackle on his football team. It didn't matter; he knew he didn't want to take the kid on in a one on one battle. Lenny looked around more, always being careful to put things back in their proper place. He was putting things back in her closet, when he heard a noise on the steps. He froze. At first he thought it was his own heart, it was beating so hard he thought for sure it would wake her son! He took a deep breath and tiptoed to the doorway and almost scared himself. It was Janice! Holy shit! His first ever night of casing a house and he gets caught by an old lady! If he did end up going to prison, the other prisoners would never let him live that down! What the hell was she doing home now!

She shouldn't be home for at least four more hours! She was coming up the steps slowly, bitching about her son leaving the light on. He had time to put the rest of what he had out, back in the closet. He quietly looked out her doorway. She had her back to him, looking in on her son. She was talking to herself. "He better be in here. Oh good he's asleep." She reclosed his door. She turned and saw Lenny and started to say something to him, but all she got out was... Lenny? In the same moment, Lenny saw his opportunity and stormed out of her room so fast he surprised her and pushed her down the full flight of stairs. He checked for a pulse, there was none. Since he was sure she was dead, he turned the hallway light off. Then he walked to his car and went home. Her son never heard anything! He couldn't believe his good fortune! Killing her like that, it definitely looked like an accident. Her head was twisted around backward. She probably broke both her legs too because they didn't look the way they should've. He knew she was dead for sure, just by looking at her. He didn't want to be near a dead body again after Mary, but he couldn't pass up that opportunity. He'll read about it in the paper or on the news. The women at work would definitely be talking...

# CHAPTER 17

Lenny got home and crawled back into bed. Cindy never even stirred. He checked her to make sure she was alive. She was breathing pretty shallow breaths. How odd he thought, I've caused two deaths and drugged my own wife to the point that I have to check her pulse. What kind of monster am I turning into? He wanted to go into work today but decided he would go to the beach house a day early with Cindy. She would love an extra day there and there had to be perks to being the boss. He was going to miss everything, all the talk in the office. It was better this way. Less suspicious. He didn't think any of the deaths had been suspicious though. He had covered his tracks so well; in his head he was thinking he could be a professional hit man. Too much stress he decided. Bill was coming to the beach house tomorrow. He would have news for him. He couldn't wait for Saturday! Bill heard about Janice's fall on the steps, but decided he was tired of Lenny ignoring his questions. So this weekend, he wasn't saying a word about it! If Lenny knew and asked him about it, Bill would know Lenny killed her. He still wasn't sure about Mary, because yesterday while

Lenny wasn't in the office all day, he snooped around. He had told Janet he needed something out of Lenny's desk. She didn't care; she knew they were old friends. She told him "go on in" He sat down in Lenny's big leather chair and looked through his massive desk. The syringes were both still in his desk drawer. Part of him thought maybe Mary did just die, the other part of him knew Lenny probably had something to do with her death. He just couldn't trust Lenny anymore. This wasn't like when they were playing ball. When he was catcher and would call a fast pitch and Lenny would throw a knuckle ball and make him look stupid for not catching it. This was serious business! He was tired of Lenny making all the rules. He needed to know what was really going on. First he asked him to help him, and then he doesn't tell him anything. He knew he was probably better off not knowing, and wanted to give Lenny the benefit of the doubt. It was hard for him to believe that Lenny could actually kill anyone. He just wanted to know so he could cover his own ass! He decided to take a woman named Kathy with him to the beach house. She was one of the women he had been dating for a couple months. He knew she liked the beach and would look awesome in a bikini. They loaded a cooler and their suitcases into his truck. He forgot he told Lenny he would bring steaks so they kept a lookout for a meat market on the way. When they found one, they both went in and decided the porterhouse steaks looked the best. They bought four of them and also bought some potatoes to throw on the grill. The store had homemade beef jerky, Bill couldn't pass that up! Kathy thought yuck! But she knew men liked that stuff. It was too salty for her. She didn't want to bloat up this weekend, in front of Bill. She was trying to snatch him for life! When they got to the beach house. Lenny and Cindy greeted them from outside in the back yard. They were right on Lake Michigan. The shore was only a hundred feet away. You could see the waves from their yard. They unloaded their things and put the steaks in the refrigerator. Cindy and Kathy wanted to go for a walk along the shore and look for shells. The guys obliged them because the waves were about three foot tall. Perfect for wave jumping. Bill and Kathy had their suits on under their clothes and Lenny and Cindy were already in their suits. They stripped down to their suits and took off for their walk, each couple hand in hand. When the girls decided they wanted to look for shells or pretty rocks, the guys were finally alone. Lenny started wave jumping and Bill jumped in right beside him. "This water is freezing "he yelled. They kept jumping though and eventually their bodies got used to the water. After half an hour they finally tired of it and went to look for the girls. While they were looking, Lenny told Bill about the sunset they would see this evening. He told him it would be outstanding. Lenny had been right about that, the sunset on Lake Michigan was spectacular! Bill didn't say a word about Janice. Lenny wanted to ask him so bad! He knew her son had to have found her. For crying out loud, she was at the bottom of the stairs! Why wasn't Bill saying anything! He figured out quick that Bill must be testing him, or he really hadn't heard anything. He hardly ever went into the lunchroom these days. Holy shit! Now he wouldn't find anything out till Monday! He wasn't giving Bill the satisfaction of asking him. Now he wished he never would have said anything to him. If he would have known how easy it was going to be, he wouldn't have said a word!

Bill was really getting on his last nerve! Then he thought maybe he just wanted a weekend of normalcy. Lenny wanted that too. They had known each other so long, Lenny had to trust him. Bill could feel Lenny getting agitated but he wasn't going to say anything that would give away that he knew about Janice. He actually didn't hear anything till he went in the lunchroom around two o'clock Friday afternoon. That's what time Janice's friends came in to work. The "retiree table" were all talking to each other and would quiet down when any low seniority people went by them. It wasn't their business I guess. They did talk to Bill though. He knew they liked him; he was always respectful to all of them. They asked him if he heard about Janice. He hadn't and he told them that. Roselle told him "she was gone; her son found her at the bottom of their stairway this morning. He had gotten up for practice and his mom must have tripped over his football bag and fallen down the steps when she got home. He didn't hear anything, he felt so bad. Poor kid. He felt like he killed his mom because he was so tired when he got home he just left his bag at the top of the stairs. He's thinking of quitting football now. I told him not to because that could be his ticket to college. I told him to stay in it for his mom. She loved going to the games and was so proud of him." Roselle knew Janice's family real well because Emily's daughters went to school with Janice's son. It was just so sad. At least he was an adult and could live on his own. Bill was as shocked as the women. People were dying on a regular basis around here. He told them "he was so sorry to hear that. He would make sure flowers were sent from corporate." He left the women to go ask Janet to order them. He always liked Janice, she wasn't in real good shape but she wanted to be. She was always asking him questions about working out. He would answer her but he did notice she never changed. She was probably just trying to make conversation with him, like a lot of the women in the office. That's too bad he thought.

# CHAPTER 18

Emily was on the phone first thing in the morning. She called her mom because her girls told her about Janice. "What happened mom?" "I don't know, I guess she fell over her son's football bag. He told me he was beat when he got home, and just left it at the top of the stairs. Poor kid." Said Roselle. Emily agreed, "Too bad she wasn't healthier, she might've been able to stop the fall," Emily said as she reminded her mom to get her butt on her stationary bike!" You could be healthier too mom!" "Yeah, yeah, yeah" Roselle answered her. They both laughed it off. Roselle hated being nagged about her health, even if they were right! They talked for a bit, then Roselle told Emily to "carry on" and they hung up.

Valerie called her that morning too. She asked the same questions that Emily had asked. Roselle was thinking she should have called them both on three way but she talked to Val for a little bit. All of her daughters knew Janice. In the summers when they were kids, the women would get together for pot luck picnics. There were so many divorced women in the place; they loved getting together with all their families. The few who did have husbands came too. Their husbands liked all the attention the women gave them. The women liked that they cooked the meat on the grill! The men didn't mind, they thought they were grill masters. Yes, those were the days, so much fun!

Roselle called Joan and Marge on three way. They needed to talk together, without all the ears from work. They couldn't believe first Carol died in her sleep then Mary at work and now Janice at home. Holy crap it's like a conspiracy they decided. Marge said "you know deaths come in threes. Hopefully this will be it for a long while." "I know" said Joan, still in shock. She was the only one of their group who had a husband. Everyone else was divorced or widowed. They did notice that all their friends who had died were alone. "Well except for Janice" said Roselle "her son was home." "Yeah but he was passed out" said Joan. "He wasn't much help. Hell he wasn't any help. That's too bad too, a big boy like that. He must feel awful!" "He does," said Roselle." I think I talked him into staying in football though. There wasn't anything he could have done. She fell, it was an accident. As much as none of us wanted that to happen, accidents do happen. That's why they call them accidents, she didn't fall on purpose!" Said Roselle

"Let's make a pact. All of us need to double check everything! Don't take anything for granted; be aware of everything going on around you! If Mary would have had an allergy pen on her or in her purse, we probably could have saved her" said Roselle. "Yes and if Janice would have turned on a light she would have seen her sons bag and not tripped over it" chimed Marge. "Yes you guys are right. Double check everything! We can't take any chances, it's like someone has it out for us soon to be retirees" said Joan. They laughed it off, but were still very serious. They made plans to go to the funeral together.

That night at work, Lenny walked around a lot but no one was talking. Roselle was giving her supervisor another graded memo. He came in and complained to Lenny. "What can I do about this" he yelled? Lenny, with a smile told him "to study his spelling and punctuation before he wrote another memo." He also reminded him Roselle would be retired soon and he wouldn't have to worry about her. "What if someone decided they need to take over her grading job" Derek asked. "Well then you write them up! You do need to study the English language Derek, or at least quit bragging about going to college!" They wouldn't pick on you so much then. I don't think any of the younger seniority will bother you. Do they even read the memos?" Lenny asked. Derek mumbled "...only to check my spelling." This made Lenny smile. "Do your homework Derek," and he ushered him out of his office.

The retirees were sitting at their table for break, Lenny walked by and heard them laughing about that dumb ass Derek. They were saying, if he wasn't so dang arrogant, they wouldn't be so hard on him. He was just a kid after all. But they couldn't stand his arrogance!

Marge told Roselle, "I can't believe you corrected another one of his memos!" Roselle said," I can't believe I had to correct another one of his memos! I was going to try and put up with it till I retired, but I just can't stand his bad grammar and poor spelling. He's always bragging about being a college graduate, he must not have taken any English classes. I can't help that I think a supervisor should know how to spell, "she said with a chuckle. "Especially one who brags so much!" She added.

Lenny called Roselle into his office. "Rosie, can you just leave Derek alone?" She was thinking maybe, if you call me by my right name! "Poor guy is getting a complex." said Lenny. "I'm sorry "she said," I told myself I was going to try to be good. It's his own fault; he knows I can't stand poor grammar. Ok ok I'll be good. I retire soon anyway, and then he can be as stupid as he wants!" Lenny looked at her like, you know if you weren't high seniority and retiring soon, I would have to give you time off. She knew it though, she was pushing her luck. She would stop. He ushered her out of his office too. Then had a good belly laugh! Yes she was going to be his hardest kill. He actually liked her. She was last though. Right now he needed to concentrate on Marge. She was his next accident waiting to happen.

He brought her name up on his computer. Wow, nothing unusual about her either, just like Janice. He still couldn't believe how lucky he was with that one. That probably wouldn't happen again in a thousand million years....

# CHAPTER 19

Roselle finally got the call from the veterinarian to come and pick Sara lee's ashes up. She called Bobbie and asked her if she wanted to ride along. "Sure mom I'll go with you." Bobbie answered. She knew how hard this was going to be on her mom. Sara Lee had been her baby. Roselle picked her up on the way there. They were riding along in the car and Bobbie asked her "what's going on at your work?" Roselle told her "it was kind of strange but people were dying off instead of retiring." Bobbie had heard about Carol a couple weeks ago when they went shopping. She also knew about Mary from when her and her mom went to breakfast last week. Emily had called Bobbie and told her about Janice. She was dumbfounded too. She watched a lot of murder mysteries on television and asked her mom "do you think someone is killing them or are they really just dying?" Roselle laughed and told her "they were just dying. Janice's death was an accident. If she would have turned a light on it probably could have been avoided. If her son would have put his bag in his room that would have helped too. You know how tired they are after football practice!" Bobbie did know because her son Josh played football too. He went to a different school but those practices were all the same. They wear them out and send them home! All Josh would do is eat and go to bed. He didn't even watch television in the evenings anymore. She could see Janice's son doing the same thing. Roselle went on talking, "Me and my friends think Mary's death might have been some kind of suicide. She knew she was allergic to pretty much everything. She used to have her allergy pen with her all the time, but she quit carrying it. We think she gave up. She hardly ever saw her grandkids, and we know she missed them. She raised her kids by herself like I did with you guys. Her kids all moved out of state though. She had to have been so lonely. I wish she would have said something, although we tried to include her with everything we did. Most of the time she didn't want to go out with us though. We thought she confided in us too, but I guess that was just too hard for her to share with us. All of us have our kids and grand kid's right here, at least within twenty five miles. I noticed in the last year when we would be talking about our grandkids, she never said anything. I mean she would say congratulations on their accomplishments but never said anything about her own grandkids. It just breaks my heart for her. Carol had died in her sleep at home. We don't know if there were extenuating circumstances or not. Sometimes God just calls you home. Sometimes I guess, it's just your time to go."

They arrived at the veterinarian's office and they both went in. Roselle knew everyone there too. She exchanged pleasantries and paid for Sara Lee's cremation. They handed her the urn of her ashes. She told them "I'm going to get another dog after I retire, pretty soon. I don't want a puppy though, maybe one that's a year old. I'm looking for a big dog. I don't like the little ones, I like real dogs!" They told her "the little ones were real too." "Yeah but they aren't as good of guard dogs" she said. They told her they would keep their eyes open for one for her. She told them thanks and to carry on, and her and Bobbie and Sara Lee left.

Bobbie said "what are you going to do with her ashes mom?" Roselle answered her "I'm not sure yet, for now I'm going to put them on my fake fireplace mantle. I could talk to the urn. At least then I won't feel like I'm crazy talking to myself all the time." They both laughed at that. Bobbie asked if she wanted to get lunch while they were out. "Sure" said Roselle. They stopped at a sandwich shop and had a quick lunch. Bobbie paid this time. She told her mom at lunch "I have to work and won't be able to go to Janice's funeral with you." Roselle told her "that's okay, I already made plans to go with Marge and Joan." "Oh good, ok. Look for the murderer. On my shows, they always go to the funerals!" Said Bobbie very seriously. Roselle rolled her eyes and reminded her it was an accident. "Whatever" said Bobbie, giving her mom the same eye roll in return.

Lenny was in his office looking up information on Marge, when Bill came in. He quickly got off that page and brought up a profit margin page. Bill wanted to thank Lenny for inviting him to the beach with him and Cindy. "That was awesome dude! I still can't get over that sunset." "I know and it's so close to home" said Lenny. "That's my favorite thing about the beach house," said Lenny.

Bill wasn't sure how to ask Lenny about the plan. He just spit it out, "So Lenny, tell me straight, have you been a part of all the deaths going on around here? What's going on?" Lenny looked at him incredulously. "Seriously! You think I could kill a person? I know we talked about that, but these women have actually helped the plan out by dying on their own" he lied. "That's good to know Lenny, I was just wondering because all of sudden we have three dead women!" Said Bill. "Since you obviously have their pension money, have you thought about using some of your own money to replace the money you took from the executive pension fund?" Asked Bill. He was really getting on Lenny's nerves now! Lenny answered him "are you kidding, maybe two more women will die accidentally!" "I'm not using my own money! They owe it to me; I gave them a job didn't I? This is my company!" Bill couldn't believe Lenny was being so arrogant. He told Lenny "there's only eight hundred thousand dollars left to replace. You could take that out of your savings!" Lenny sent him out of his office "go find someone to flirt with Bill, you're out of line!" Before he left he told Lenny "I can't believe you've turned into such a greedy bastard! Your dad, who by the way still owns this company, would be ashamed!!" Then he stormed out of the office...

# CHAPTER 20

Lenny was furious now, the nerve of Bill! Who did he think he was talking to! I'd fire his ass right now but he knows too much! He should've known Bill would bring his dad in to the conversation. His dad would want an explanation if he fired him. Lenny always felt like his dad liked Bill more than he did him. His dad always had to take Bill with them wherever they went. Why wasn't it enough to just take me, he often wondered. He always thought his dad felt sorry for Bill. His parents never had any spare money. Bills parents were the fun ones though, his dad coached them in little league. He was always involved with whatever they were doing. They would take him to the pizza place with them after games. His own parents were too busy to go to most of the games, let alone get pizza! Lenny loved Bills parents. He knew they were good people. He knew he would forgive Bill; they have just been through too much together. He just didn't know when! Even though his dad didn't ask about the company anymore, he did always ask how Bill was doing. He knew he would have to forgive him eventually, or lie to his dad! When does it end?

When can he go back to being himself again? Was this the new him? Liar, Cheater, Killer???

Greedy my ass! This was my company and if anyone is keeping their money, it would be me! I'm not giving up a penny of my bonus! These women were going to pay for my mistakes, not me! I'm the freaking president of this company! I own them!! Executives deserved their bonuses, we earn them! These women who worked for him were just pawns in his game now.

Now more than ever, he wasn't telling Bill anything more. He realized it was probably a big mistake telling Bill anything, and wished he wouldn't have said a word! He really hadn't told him much anyway, just what he needed to do and that was about the money. He never came right out and said he was going to kill anyone. He wasn't going to give him any more evidence he could possibly use against him. Just talking wasn't evidence! People all the time were saying... I could've killed that guy. So far all the deaths had been perfectly planned. Well Janice wasn't planned but that was perfect timing. The police couldn't pinpoint anything on him. Mary had been cremated and if they dug up Janice's body, they wouldn't find any evidence there either. The only thing Bill could get him for was the embezzlement. He didn't think Bill had the balls to tell the police though. It would be like turning in your brother! He would be cordial with Bill, just in case. He actually thought Bill owed him an apology. The nerve of some people, give them everything and they want more!

Bill went back to his office, he was mad as hell. Lenny had turned into a corporate creep. The ones they talk about on television. So this is what they meant by corporate greed. The gall of Lenny to say he owned these women!

Bill didn't grow up with a silver spoon in his mouth like Lenny had. His parents worked for everything they owned. Both his parents worked hard their whole lives! Nothing was ever handed to them. What if his mom were one of these women! She could have easily been any one of these women! If her boss decided he wanted to steal from her pension fund, and kill her before she could get it, he would be furious! Hell, he was furious, he just couldn't prove anything! Even though Lenny's parents took Bill on vacations with them and helped him get through college. He didn't owe Lenny crap! He would always respect his parents, but Lenny just blew any respect he ever had for him! He might not have any evidence for murder but he knew about the embezzlement and that was a crime! He wasn't going to tell the police though because Lenny didn't deserve to go to a federal prison and have it easy, he needed to go to a state prison where he would have to fight to survive. Part of him felt like, if they really were accidents and he got the money that way, it was kind of okay. The man was like a brother to him even if he was pissed as hell at him right now. The other part of him thought he was a class A asshole and deserved to be turned in to the police! He didn't know what he was going to do. He wasn't sure if he could do that to Cindy. She certainly didn't deserve any of this heartache.

Lenny was on his computer looking through Marge's file. There wasn't anything unusual on her file, just like Janice's file. He was concerned because he knew he was really lucky with that one. He had wanted to wait another week before he killed another one, but he couldn't pass up that opportunity. He thought to himself, could he get that lucky again? That would be awesome, the way it was working out, they couldn't point anything at him. If he could kill all four of them and make it look like an accident, he would get away with it. He couldn't even imagine that, could he? He has turned into a monster, but he was good at it. His conscious wasn't happy but he felt like he would deal with that later. Didn't psychologists have a doctor - client privilege? He wasn't sure if he would ever tell anyone but he wasn't sure if he could keep it to himself forever either.

He was going to have to case Marge's house too. He got lucky once maybe it will happen again. He could always hope. He memorized her address and planned on driving past it on his way home tonight...

# CHAPTER 21

Even though Lenny memorized Marge's address, he didn't have a clue where it was. When he looked it up on his map website on his computer, he saw it wasn't in a good area of town. He thought to himself, crap I don't know if I want to go in that neighborhood at night! Her neighborhood was in the news all the time for shootings. There were drug deals going on there too. It was close to work though. He was going to have to figure this out. She had lived there for fifty years, raised her kids there and probably knew everyone around her. He wondered why she stayed in that neighborhood. He paid his employees well; there wasn't any reason for her to have to live there! This one was going to be harder than he had thought at first.

He left work early because he wanted to go past her house the first time in the daylight. Holy crap, just getting close scared him. Sure you're big and bad, you already killed two women, old women, but still, he thought to himself as he drove further into her neighborhood. He could see groups of teenagers on the corners. They had jackets on and it wasn't cold enough for a jacket. For Pete's sake, it's close to eighty degrees outside! Why the hell were they wearing jackets? He wondered if it was some kind of gang thing. They probably had guns inside their jackets! They had bandannas tied on their heads too. They all looked like pretty shady characters to him. This area was known for its gang problems. He was truly scared for his own life. What am I afraid of? Hell I've killed two people! These kids didn't know who they were dealing with! He tried to pump himself up. It worked for a little while. Yep I'm scared shitless, I'm getting the hell out of here! He said to himself. He thought, maybe they go to bed and two o'clock in the morning might be better. Crap Marge didn't work the all night shift though. He was going to have to schedule her for it. Then he could try this again, these kids had to go to bed sometime! Didn't they have to get up for school he wondered? He went on home, anything to get out of there. He got home kind of early, but Cindy was happy to have him home. She made spaghetti for supper and they had a nice quiet evening at home. It was strange but, when he was home, he felt like a normal guy. The kind of guy who worked on stuff in his garage. The kind of guy who mowed his own lawn. The kind of guy who would never gamble with other people's money. The kind of guy who would never cheat on his wife. The kind of guy who wasn't capable of killing anyone. Then he would remember that he had killed two women, and gambled with others money and for Pete's sake cheated on his wife! He had to get through all this guilt. He wondered if he was getting schizophrenia. One guy at home, a completely different guy when he was planning a murder. He reminded himself of a tee shirt he once saw, it said: I'm schizophrenic and so am I. That brought a smile to his lips. Did that qualify him as a schizophrenic, he wondered. He wasn't hearing voices though, did you have to hear voices he wondered. On television, it seemed like they always heard voices. If he gets caught, he decided he would plead insanity. Then he could go to a mental hospital, they might be able to help him with the guilt too.

The next day he looked in the computer to see if anyone else lived in that area. The cleaning lady, Sue lived kind of close to that neighborhood. He stayed at work later than what was considered normal. He wanted to talk to Sue. She finally came in to work. She worked for herself and not the company. He let her clean for awhile till most of the women were out of the lunchroom. Then he approached her and asked her how things were going. "Fine sir" she answered. He small talked for awhile with her. Then he dove right in and asked her about gangs in her neighborhood. She told him the gangs were awful. She also told him "those kids are out all damn night .I don't think they even go to school! They're always out on the corners, scaring every decent person in the neighborhood, always up to no good!" "Why do you still live there then," he asked her. She told him "mostly because my house isn't worth what I would need to get out of there plus it's paid for. My neighbors and I look out for each other, we know when there's a strange car driving around. Some of the neighbors even keep track of those license plate numbers, just in case the police need them. None of us go out at night or answer our doors after dark either. We check on each other too. The police don't hurry up and get there if we call them at night either. It's really sad how bad it's gotten on that side of town; it used to be really nice. We used to have mostly older people and families, but when they died, slumlords bought the properties up and they don't care who they rent to. Now even the families that were there have moved out. Anyone who could get out has gotten out!" She said. Well crap he thought to himself. He was going to have to change his plan. Sue talked him right out of that idea. He still for the life of him couldn't understand why Marge stayed in that area of town! It just didn't make any sense. It didn't sound like it was ever going to be safe to go in Marge's neighborhood either, no matter what time it was! Damn!

# CHAPTER 22

Roselle was starting to get really excited about retiring. She and Marge both were getting excited. Joan still had a couple more years till she could retire. She was going to miss these guys though. Two more years and Joan was out of there too. She and her husband were going to retire at the same time. Marge only had two weeks left and Roselle had a month. They had worked together forever. They all were in their twenties when they started there and now were all in their fifties. Marge was a little older but they all started around the same time and became friends. They couldn't believe how fast the time went, seems like they just started working. They had a lot of memories from this place. A lot of memories together. Joan wondered if any of their kids were planning a retirement party for them. She decided she would call Bobbie, Roselle's daughter, tonight when she got home. She was the one she figured who would plan Roselle's party. Bobbie was the one who could change her schedule when Roselle broke her ankle a few years ago. She would take her to the doctor appointments. She also did a wheelie with Roselle in her wheelchair. They always had so much fun when they were together. She took after her mom the most out of all of her girls. She looked like her and acted like her. I bet they talk to everyone they see when they're together, she thought with a smile.

Bobbie was planning a retirement party. She called Emily and Valerie to see if they had any ideas. Emily wanted to have it at a restaurant and Valerie wanted to do a picnic in the park. Bobbie just wanted to get everyone together with good food and music that mom liked. She kind of wanted it to be a surprise, but not a loud surprise. She knew from taking her mom to the doctor so much a couple years ago, that she had congestive heart disease. She didn't tell her sisters because mom didn't want her to. Mom said she would tell them. So she let it go. She didn't want her having a heart attack at her own retirement party! That would totally spoil the mood! Between the three of them, they decided to have it at the Mexican restaurant they all liked. Emily, the proverbial first born always got her way. Valerie and Bobbie weren't happy about it, but agreed to it. There just wasn't any sense in arguing with Emily. She was right; it would be easier for setting up and cleaning up. They had good food too. They had free appetizers too with the chips and salsa. Everybody liked free stuff! Bobbie told them she would call the place and reserve their party room. Mom was retiring on her fifty-eighth birthday. They decided it could be a combination party. "Ask them if we can decorate the room too "Valerie said. Emily said, "We need to know if we can bring our own cake too." Bobbie told them, "ok ok I'll be sure to ask them all of that stuff, plus I want to know if they have any way to play some music." "This is going to be a lot of fun you guys!" Said Bobbie. Emily and Val agreed and made plans to get together to discuss the party more. They said their goodbyes and hung up with each other.

Bobbie called the restaurant and asked about reserving the party room. They had an opening the day after moms birthday. They also told her they could decorate the room and bring their own cake. The music would be a little different because they had Latino music piped in throughout the whole restaurant. Bobbie figured she would just bring her CD player, it played tapes too. They could have it on in one corner of the room, not too loud and ask the restaurant to turn their music down in the party room. The day after mom's birthday was close enough for her. It would definitely be a surprise. She would just tell mom that she and Tj would pick her up and take her out to dinner for her birthday. She wouldn't suspect a thing. She might think Valerie and Jim and Emily and Cam would be there, but she would never think all her friends would be there too. Bobbie needed to call Joan. She could tell people at moms work when mom wasn't around. She could tell Marge too. Next Monday when they went to volunteer at the soup kitchen, Bobbie would tell them too. Mom was going to be so surprised! This was so much fun planning a party for her! When Bobbie went to work that evening, she was sitting with two of her friends, Jackie and Collette, they had some ideas too. Jackie said "they should have`a piñata since it was at the Mexican restaurant." Collette piped in "maybe not, I wouldn't want to give a bunch of blindfolded old people a big stick, it could be dangerous!" They all laughed at that comment! Bobbie said "yeah we might have to think about that." Well they would have to be supervised by someone without a blindfold" said Jackie. "That's true, and you could have the piñata in the shape of a big telephone" said Collette. The three of them had worked together for a few years and had gotten to be great friends. Jackie, like Bobbie was married and had two daughters. She was a small woman, but don't ever cross her, she'll let you have it. Jackie never backed down from anyone. She was tough as nails when she needed to be and soft as a baby other times. People respected her opinions and often asked for them. Collette was a whole different story. She was single and liked to date as many men as she could. Bobbie and Jackie lived vicariously through her. They loved hearing about her "flavors of the week!" Collette considered herself to be the most experienced of the three, and always told of her escapades with all her "chocolate thunders" She was a tall, proud, voluptuous, black woman. She had men come in to the store just to talk to her! She had a big heart though and Jackie and Bobbie loved her. As good as their ideas were, Bobbie knew she would have to talk it over with Emily and Valerie.

Lenny had to think of a different plan. Anything at Marge's house was out of the question! He wasn't stepping a foot in that neighborhood ever again! He truly didn't know how Marge and Sue both lived there. Maybe he could pay someone to set the whole neighborhood on fire, he thought. Then that side of town could start all over again. No that wouldn't work! As mad as he was at Bill, he was right about one thing. Don't get too many people involved. If he hired an arsonist, that would be a witness and he couldn't afford any witnesses. He was so close to cleaning up the mess he made with the executive pension fund. There hasn't even been any suspicion on him or anyone else! He was on too good of a roll to involve anyone else. He didn't want to ask Bill either! He needed some ideas, maybe poison he thought. He needed to go to the library because he didn't want to have that on his internet browser at work or at home.

On his lunch break, he walked to the library. It was right by the office, how convenient he thought. He walked in and was as invisible as a ghost. Everyone at the library was working on their own projects. No one even noticed him. This was perfect for anonymity. He logged onto the computer as a guest and looked up poisons. Sodium cyanide would do it, but that was too quick. He didn't want to have another death happen right at work. He didn't want to be anywhere close when it happened. Arsenic would do it too. He could probably get hold of that easier than cyanide. It's in rat poison. He decided to go to the hardware store on his way home. He already thought about what he would tell the store if they asked. There actually were rats in the parking lot sometimes. He wouldn't have to lie. He was growing weary of the lying and conniving, and killing, but it didn't stop him. He knew he wasn't finished yet. The hardest was yet to come...

# CHAPTER 23

The sisters all decided to meet for lunch to talk about mom's party. Bobbie was telling Valerie and Emily about her friend's piñata idea. They both liked it; the party was at a Mexican restaurant. It would match the decor of the place! However, Emily was concerned; she didn't want it to be like a little kids party. It won't, Bobbie and Valerie promised her. They looked at each other with big smiles. Emily could be such a party pooper sometimes! "Mom will be so freakin surprised you guys" said Bobbie. She was really getting excited for the party and for their mom to retire! She had worked their whole lives and really deserved to retire. Bobbie said "hey, I want to invite some of my friends too." Emily chimed in "it's not your party Bobbie." Valerie said "How about we each invite two friends and their spouses?" "Then we'll have our own big table and mom can have the rest of the room" said Bobbie. Emily took charge and told them, "first we need to know how many of moms friends are coming, then we need to know how many can be in the room according to fire code, then we can decide if we can invite friends." Bobbie and Valerie looked at each other and said at the same time "party pooper", but they knew she was right. They just liked ganging up on her. Bobbie already invited Jackie and her husband and Collette and her man. If they had to, they could have dinner in the main dining room and Bobbie would walk through on her way to the bathroom, and see them, coincidentally of course, and ask them to come for cake. She had it all figured out, but she wasn't telling Emily! Nobody said, you had to tell your big sister everything! She would be mad, mostly because she didn't think of it first. What she doesn't know won't hurt her Bobbie thought with a smile. Bobbie told them "I'm going to have Tj's cousin, Lori, make the cake. She could make one in the shape of an old fashioned phone, with a couple extension phones if they needed more cake. We could even have different flavored cake for the extension phones. Mom and the ladies she worked with would love it!" Emily said "have you ever had her cake? I don't like that frosting crap, I want butter cream icing." "Lori can make whichever kind we want, and yes I've tasted her cake. It's the best cake ever! You're going to love it Emily!" Said Bobbie. Valerie didn't care, she knew she would have to run those calories off whichever icing it had. Bobbie asked them "do either of you guys know anyone who makes piñata's?" Emily said "yes my friend, Maria might make it. I'll have to ask her though". Bobbie told her "to get busy on it because paper mâché takes a while, each layer had to dry." "I want candy inside it too. Chocolate candy said Valerie. If she was going to have to run, might as well make it a marathon she thought.

Lenny started thinking, maybe he could get rid of someone else. Marge was really becoming a problem, and he actually liked Roselle. Then he reminded himself, that he wanted to get it done now! Marge and Roselle were the only ones left who weren't taking care of a special needs child and lived alone. He never realized how many physically and mentally challenged kids were out there, and it seemed like most of their moms worked for him! Some of the women who were retiring soon didn't have spouses but he knew they had roommates. Ugh it was going to have to be these two. Okay just get it done and you won't have to worry about it. He wondered how healthy Marge's heart was. Maybe she'll have a heart attack and save him the trouble he thought. That would be so nice and helpful! He was still at the library and decided to look up if there was a way to make someone have a heart attack with chemicals that weren't poisonous. Holy crap! He found an article on potassium chloride. Amazing, he thought to himself. The person would have a heart attack but the coroner would only find chemicals that are already in their body! Oh my God, that's just what I need! He proceeded to read the article. It said he would have to get hold of a doctor's prescription pad. That might be hard, he hated going to the doctor! He read on further and found out it was a salt substitute. Hmm how could he make this work? The article was updated further down as he kept reading. He found out he could get it from a health food store, that he didn't have to go to the doctor. Wow that's progress he thought. Holy crap he was starting to get that inner excitement again! He looked up health food stores and saw there was one in the mall a few towns away. He didn't want to go to his local mall, because he didn't want to take a chance on running into anyone he knew. He didn't want to go to the mall in the town Cindy's parents were in either. He never knew if her mom and dad would be out shopping. Yeah he definitely didn't want to go to their town. They knew everyone! He knew what his plan was now. He shut the computer down and went back to his office. His lunchtime was over anyway. He didn't like being late from lunch because the ladies would see him and think that's pretty crappy. You make us punch out for lunch and you take half the day. Imagine what they would think if they knew he killed Mary and Janice...

# CHAPTER 24

Lenny stopped and got a candy bar out of the machine in the lunchroom. Yes he had the regular brown nosers coming up to him as soon as he walked in. He didn't know why they insisted on asking him the same questions over and over again. Sometimes he wished he could kill them all. He would fantasize about that some other time. Right now he had other things to concentrate on. He needed to check the schedule to see when Marge worked this week. He was definitely going to the mall after work tonight to get his potassium chloride. He was so happy because this wasn't a poison and just something a lot of people bought every day. He started to wonder why there were any assholes left on earth, when it would be so easy to get rid of all of them! If people only knew what they could do with this stuff. He knew he was going to have to get rid of Cindy for an evening too. The potassium chloride would have to be in a concentrated liquid form for what he had in mind. If anyone can take twenty milligrams every day, he was going to have to make it at least one hundred milligrams to take care of the job. It would be nice if Marge was taking a water pill too. He remembered something in the article about side effects if you were taking a water pill. Marge was old, compared to him, actually compared to the women she hung around with too. She was in her sixties, so he figured she probably took something for blood pressure and cholesterol. The more side effects the better he thought. He would need something to calm his nerves too, if he lived in her neighborhood.

He was looking at reports on his computer when Cindy called him. "Hi baby" she said. He answered her "Hi honey, what's up? You don't usually call me at work, is something wrong?" "Well, you mean other than my mom twisting her ankle and my dad having a fishing trip planned in Canada" she said. "Oh no! Is she going to be all right? You need to go over there don't you? Do you want me to take a couple days off and go with you? "He asked. "You don't have to go with me baby, but I appreciate the offer" she said while smiling to herself. "Dads trip is for the whole week though, will you be ok for that long?" She asked. "Of course, I'll be fine. I can maybe come up during the week for the evening, and take you and your mom out to supper. You're only gonna be seventy miles away" he told her. "That would be sweet, mom would like that" she said. Cindy went on "I'm going to go up today so dad can finish getting packed for his trip without worrying about mom, ok baby". "Sure "he answered, "call me when you get there. I love you!" "I will and I love you too!" She answered

Wow! It was like he was supposed to be planning murders. Everything just falls into place. Now he would be able to go to the health food store, and cook his potassium chloride to a deadly concentrated liquid. He wasn't going to have to worry about Cindy interfering for the whole week! That was outstanding he thought to himself. He would have to remember to get off early one afternoon and take her and her mom out to supper.

Back to work, he needed to make a list. Number one on the list was potassium chloride, whatever form they had it in. If it was already in liquid form, it wouldn't be as strong as he was going to need it to be. He really was hoping for pill form.

Number two on the list was olive oil, but he was sure Cindy had that in their kitchen. He had seen some when he made chicken noodle soup a couple weeks ago. Hopefully there was some left in the cabinet. If not though, it would be easy to pick up at the grocery store.

Number three on the list was antifreeze. He most likely had some in the garage. If he didn't, just like olive oil, it would be nothing to pick some up at the store. He only needed a drop of it anyway.

Number four on the list was to remember to take the syringes home.

So far that's it he thought. He couldn't think of anything else he would need right away. He put the syringes in his jacket pocket while he was thinking about it. He definitely didn't want to forget them!

Bill was on vacation this week and Lenny was glad too. He was still super pissed at him. He hadn't apologized for suggesting that Lenny use his own money to pay back the fund. What an asshole! Lenny thought!

He hadn't checked the schedule yet. So he was walking towards the bulletin board by the locker room, through the lunchroom.

As Lenny walked through the lunchroom, and passed the "retiree table". Roselle, and Marge, and Joan were just getting ready to sit down. They were laughing and talking, like they were girls in college. He never noticed but all the women in here were wearing sweaters. Mary had a lot of sweaters in her locker too, he remembered from her daughter coming in and cleaning out her locker. He usually had a suit coat on so he liked it cooler. He didn't realize he was freezing everyone out. Oh well he thought, they're probably all in menopause anyway. They don't know what temperature they want it. He thought with a smile. He noticed the women were picking up dog bones off the floor. He couldn't help himself and bent over to get down where they were and said "you ladies know we have real food here ... Right". They all laughed and Marge told him

"they were Roselle's; they fell out of her pocket". Lenny laughed and walked over to the schedule, but on the inside he was thinking... Son of a bitch! She has a dog...

# CHAPTER 25

Lenny was looking at the schedule nonchalantly. He quickly saw that Marge worked all this week. She worked the mid day shift too. Awesome he thought! Next Friday was her last day. Everyone there was happy for her and congratulating her every chance they had. To Lenny, it was a deadline! The stairwell door was right by the schedule, so he took the stairs. Sometimes that was the only exercise he would get all day. They were on the sixth floor of the building and he felt that it was enough of a workout. He would never be as buff as Bill and he was okay with that. He didn't need women hitting on him, he was already married to the woman he wanted. He hated walking up the steps but he never minded going down them. He walked out to his car without talking to anyone else. He didn't know where the guard was. He was ok with it though. The guy probably had to use the bathroom. Lord knows he's probably older than all these women. Prostrate problems run rampant at his age. If he could put up with the women and their menopause then this guy could go to the freakin bathroom whenever he needed to! Everyone who worked there knew the code to get into the building. It was for their safety. If they only knew, Lenny was the one they needed to be afraid of. They wouldn't give a crap about that door and its code!

The women were planning a retiree party for all of them. Something for at work. They decided to have a pot- luck carry in. They had so many different nationalities working there, that it would be crazy not to do a carry in. They decided to do it by seniority. One year through five years would bring desserts. Six through ten years would bring a casserole. Eleven through fifteen would bring a salad or drinks. Sixteen through twenty five would bring a meat dish. Twenty six through thirty three would bring plates, silverware and cups and napkins. Everyone decided if they had that much seniority, they shouldn't have to cook! It was going to be delicious. That was going to be this week on Wednesday before Marge and Roselle retired.

Lenny finally walked down all those stairs and to his car. He was headed to the mall out of town. He was also glad Cindy wasn't with him because she liked to shop too much. He just wanted to run in, get the stuff and leave. He knew he was going to have to do some cooking too. He needed to combine this stuff. He wasn't going to think about that till he saw what form the store had it in. He hoped it was pill form, so he could make it strong. This is going to be perfect. According to the article the repercussions wouldn't be right away. Hopefully they wouldn't take effect until Marge got home from work. She lived alone, and he didn't know how often her kids visited. Lenny knew he was taking a chance that she wouldn't make it home. He didn't have a choice though. He had to do it this way, because he was too chicken to go in her neighborhood again.

He pulled up to the mall and parked his car, and walked in the door. He didn't know where the store was located in here, but they had a "you are here" map. Walking over to it, he noticed the mall was really crowded. Then he remembered school starts pretty soon. These were back to school shoppers. Moms and kids and grandmas and grand kids. It didn't matter to him, as long as the mall was packed! No one even noticed the man in the nice suit going to the health food store. That's the way he wanted it too. Everything just seemed to work out perfectly for him. It made him feel like this was his destiny, to be a killer, it was just too freaking easy!

He found the store he needed, and walked in. He began to look for his potassium chloride and couldn't find it anywhere. This place was packed full with bottles of stuff that all looked the same! Finally an employee asked him if he needed any help. "Yes I do" he answered. He told the guy what he needed and the kid took him right to it. Lenny thought to himself, is this kid even old enough to work? The older he got the younger eighteen year olds looked. After he told the employee thank you, the kid left him alone to make his choice. They had ten milligrams, and twenty milligram tablets. Perfect! He thought. He was thrilled they had it in pill form. He didn't want to have to mess with the liquid. He grabbed the twenty milligram bottle and headed to the checkout. While he was checking out, the employee looked at what he had and told him "you're only going to need one of these a day. Don't take any more than that in one day". Lenny lied and said "I know, I've taken them before, but thank you!" He paid cash and got out of the mall. He couldn't tell the kid, oh no problem I'm just using them to kill an employee. He laughed to himself. He was a devious soul, what was happening to him? He didn't know but was glad he was able to carry out his plan.

Getting out of the parking lot without getting hit was another problem. Too many grandmas with lots of money. They drove like they owned the parking lot! They kept giving him that look that said "don't make me get out of this car and smack you" He let them have their way because he didn't want to bring any attention to himself. It took him ten minutes just to get out of the parking lot. He started to drive home and on the way stopped and bought a sandwich from the sandwich shop close to his house. He got it "to go" and took it home with him. He had work to do...

# CHAPTER 26

When he got home, he changed his clothes and put some comfy clothes on. Shorts and a t shirt were so much more comfortable. He noticed the blinker on the answering machine was blinking. He played the message; it was Cindy letting him know she made it to her parent's house. He called her back real quick just to let her know he loved her. He told her it was a long day and he was just going to eat and watch the ball game. They said their I love you's and hung up. Then he ate his sandwich, while reading the label on the bottle of potassium chloride. The information on the bottle made him think twice about salt and salt substitutes in his and Cindy's diet. After he ate, he grabbed a small pan from the cabinet and two spoons out of the drawer. He was going to smash the pills between the spoons, over the pan so he wouldn't have any mess. The article he read said that when this is given intravenously, bypassing the digestive tract, thirty milligrams was a lethal dose. They even use this in the prisons for death row inmates. Lenny secretly hoped he would never have to find out about it in prison. How ironic that what the state used to lethally inject prisoners was how he was using it too.

He wasn't going to put it in her vein, like at the prisons, so he ground up five tablets into the pan. Then added some olive oil, and mixed it real well. He put that on the stove on the lowest possible flame. Then he had to run out to the garage and get the antifreeze. When he came back inside it was already simmering. He then added just one drop of antifreeze. He didn't want her dying anywhere inside the building. He let that cook down till he had enough for the syringes. He noticed that there wasn't any odor from it either. It also cooked down really well too. Look ma no lumps he thought with a smile. He truly didn't understand how he could smile about this crap! He had gotten so cavalier about death in the last month. "Part of the deal dude" he said aloud to himself. Then he carefully filled each syringe and put the cap on so they wouldn't leak. He cleaned up the kitchen, making sure he got that pan sparkling clean. He wasn't taking any chances on Cindy or himself getting sick. That would put suspicion on himself he thought. Then he went in the living room to watch some baseball. This is when he missed Bill. He was his favorite friend to watch a game with. It reminded him of the games they played together, from little league all the way through college. He decided then he was going to let this thing with Bill blow over. He couldn't stand not having his best friend around. He wasn't going to tell him the truth though. It was pretty obvious that Bill couldn't handle it. He really wished he wouldn't have said anything at all about it to him. A month ago, he didn't realize what his options were and thought he needed help. Damn! I could kick myself in the ass for telling him!

Emily called Bobbie and told her Maria said yes to making the piñata. "She said she can make it the shape of a phone too" "awesome" said Bobbie. She also told Emily "the cake is going to be carrot cake with cream cheese butter cream icing." Emily said "oh yeah mom will like that, we know she likes cream cheese! Remember the chip dip with horseradish and cream cheese she always made." Bobbie told her "of course I do! That's what made me think of a carrot cake" they both laughed. I make that chip dip too; my kids and Tj all love it. They weren't rich growing up. Matter of fact, some of the married women who had two incomes and teenage daughters, would bring clothes in for them. They didn't mind, it was nice getting some cool clothes. They didn't have a lot but they always had each other. They had memories of going to the drive in, and picnics in the park, and even though mom couldn't swim she made sure they all could. Mom hated that she couldn't swim. She would never go on a cruise like Emily wanted for her. Bobbie told Emily "I'm going to tell mom that me and Tj will pick her up and take her out for a birthday supper. You and Cam and Val and Jim go to the restaurant and set up the surprise." Emily asked her "do you think mom will recognize her friend's cars in the parking lot?" Bobbie said "no, it's a huge parking lot. It should be okay". Emily asked Bobbie "are you getting a lot of responses to the invitations? Did you tell them it's a surprise?" Bobbie said. "Yes I'm getting a lot of responses, even the women who are our age. I definitely told them it's a surprise, plus Joan is telling some of the women we don't know. I told the people at the soup kitchen last Monday too. A lot of them are coming too. They were pretty excited about it. I can't wait Emily!!" "It's really starting to look like a party" Said Emily. "Yes it is" answered Bobbie. They talked a little longer about Emily's new house and her upholstery business. Bobbie told her "let me know when they have the walls and roof finished, so we can come out and look at it." Every time she talked to Emily she made it seem like it was almost finished. The first time her and Tj went to see it, it was just a hole in the ground! They thought they were going to see at least a basement from the way Emily was talking about it. Oh well it would get finished and they could see it then. Right now Bobbie was too busy with mom's party anyway.

# CHAPTER 27

Lenny left the syringes at home this morning. With Cindy at her parents, he knew he didn't have to worry about her seeing them. He needed to follow Marge at least once, maybe a couple times. He had to learn her habits. He was sure she took the elevator. She was too old to take the stairs. He knew, by looking at the schedule, she was leaving at seven tonight. Cindy not being home really helped him out. The carry in the women planned was tomorrow. He planned on leaving early then and driving to Cindy's parents. He told her he would come up and take the two of them out to supper. He wanted Marge to enjoy the carry in because it was going to be like a last supper for her. Look at me playing God he thought. God will surely strike me down! I better not even think that! He was getting pretty brave in his own head. Everything seemed more rational in his head. If it wasn't supposed to happen, why was it so easy, everything just fell right into place for him.

When he walked through the lunchroom today, they were all talking about what they were bringing. He didn't come in till eleven because he knew he was staying till seven. The lunch crowd was already in there. It really was a good group of women. Those girls that flirted with Bill all the time in human resources had done a good job hiring these ladies. Kudos to them he thought.

He was reading his reports, when one of his executives knocked on his door jamb. "It's open come on in "he told the guy. "What's up" Lenny asked? The guy started telling him about cellular service and phones and the profit they could make if they went into the cellular business. Lenny had already heard it from Bill. Lenny told the guy "look it's nineteen ninety six, if everyone was going to be carrying a cellular phone, it would've happened by now! It's never going to happen! People will always have to have a phone in their house!" The guy, knowing Lenny's mind was closed to the idea respectfully disagreed and left Lenny's office. "where does this guy get off! "He thought. People are never going to each have their own phone! It would be nice for profits but it wasn't going to happen. Next thing they're going to come in and tell me is they can put a computer in their phone too. He had to laugh at himself for even thinking that one! Cellular telephones were on the market but they were so clunky and costly. The average consumer couldn't afford one. He couldn't believe anyone would want to be that accessible all the time. People would be talking while they're driving, holy crap what a mess that would be. It was hard enough concentrating on the road while you're changing the radio station or putting a different tape in the tape player. Some newer cars were coming out with CD players. That was an improvement he liked. You didn't have to worry about having a screwdriver in the car to wind tapes that messed up. He could imagine the accidents it would cause with teenage drivers. They already were at a disadvantage because they lacked experience. He called Janet into his office. He asked her" did you hear that guy?" She told him "yes I did, can you imagine if everywhere we went we had a telephone! Crap, I would never get anything done; my kids would be calling me all the time! No thank you!" Lenny said "I know! It would be good for profits, but it's not conceivable. There would have to be huge towers everywhere and scientists say they cause Cancer too. No one would want a tower near them. If it was going to happen I think it would have happened by now" Janet agreed "I don't want a phone on me all the time, and then it would start to control you. You wouldn't be able to screen your calls either. Just not possible or plausible!" They both laughed about it. Janet asked him "do you need anything Lenny?" He told her "no I'm fine, thanks for coming in and letting me know you feel the same way I do about cellular phones" she told him "no problem" and went back to her desk. It was almost five and she had filing to finish up before she left for the day.

After Janet left, Lenny went to the lunchroom to see if there were any treats in there. Yay he thought there's some kind of cake in there. The cleaning lady, Sue, told him it was called better than sex cake. Well he thought to himself, with Cindy at her parents, this was the closest he was going to get to sex this week. He helped himself to a piece. Mmmm it was good, he wasn't sure if it was better than sex but it was a close second! He took his plate back to his office to finish it while he worked. It was getting close to six thirty and he knew he wanted to walk down with Marge. He finished up everything he had been working on. Shut his desktop computer down and just waited in his office till five minutes to seven. Then he sauntered into the lunchroom, saw Marge at the" retiree table" getting her things together. He started talking to her about what her plans were after she retires. They started walking towards the elevator as she told him she was just planning on spending more time with her family and grandkids. All he really heard was blah, blah, blah. He wasn't really paying attention to anything she said. What he did notice is, they were the only ones in the elevator. That would be perfect if that happened Thursday too. He also noticed she parked in the back lot. He walked with her to her car and noticed which one it was. He was planning on parking as close as he could to it on Thursday. He was thinking you don't even know what's coming...

# CHAPTER 28

Today was the day of the carry in. The ladies never expected Lenny to bring anything. They really just hoped that he liked what they brought. Lenny went to work early because he knew he was going to be leaving by four today. It was an hour and a half drive to Cindy's parents. That would get him there around five thirty. Perfect time for supper he thought. Then he could leave and get home by nine, even nine thirty would be okay.

He walked in through the lunchroom, wow! He couldn't believe all the food there already. There were even some breakfast casseroles. Mmm that sounded good. He helped himself as ladies were telling him "try mine Lenny." He really enjoyed good food and would try everything if his stomach would let him. Having Cindy out of town was inconvenient for his meals, so he thought it was perfect timing for the women to bring all this home cooked goodness in! He figured he would try not to eat too much because he was going out to supper tonight. It wouldn't hurt if he ate a big breakfast though, so he filled his plate. Then he took it to his office to eat every bite. He was hungry; all he ate for supper last night was another sandwich from the place by his house.

The women were excited about the carry in. It was the one time they could show off their cultures food. Homemade enchiladas, and burritos, and clam chowder. Plus your usual carry in stuff. Macaroni and cheese, broccoli and rice, and don't forget the meatballs! Anything you could want, they had it, cakes, baklava, pies, just everything! Everyone who was on a diet went off of it today. Since different seniority dates worked each shift, you had a complete meal, even in the morning. Everyone was taking longer than normal breaks especially the ladies that already signed retirement papers. They figured, what did they have to lose, they would be out of there soon enough.

The mid afternoon shift came in and it was a whole new wave of different food. Marge was in this group. She only had to bring paper products though with her seniority. Roselle and Joan were scheduled at four o'clock. They were working the night shift, but would see the mid shift people. The women had two eight foot tables full of paper products and drinks and food. Even the women were surprised at the variety of good food. This was the biggest carry in they had ever pulled off. Everyone participated. Lenny was regretting having to drive to Cindy's parent's house tonight. He ate so freaking much food already today! He might just have soup or a salad tonight. He knew he wasn't going to be too hungry. Hell with all the food he ate, he might not get hungry again until Friday!

Lenny was thinking eat up Marge! This was your last big meal. The anticipation was driving him crazy!

Roselle stopped at Bobbies on her way to work. She didn't

get supper though; she told her they were having a carry in today. She probably wouldn't eat healthy either. Grunt got his peanut butter bone from her and went to eat it. She loved him. She told Bobbie about the bones falling out of her pocket at work. Her and her friends were laughing about it as they picked them up from the floor, and her boss telling her they had real food. She was so animated telling her story to Bobbie that they both started laughing. Work could be fun; Bobbie always had a good time with her friends at work too. Roselle and Bobbie talked about getting some bulbs for fall flower planting. Bobbie told her she has a friend who has a greenhouse. Her name was Carmel and she would most likely give them a good deal too. They planned a trip to her greenhouse for over the weekend. Bobbie wanted to get some tulip bulbs. Roselle didn't want tulips but wanted to look at all she has in stock, and then decide. It was so hard for Bobbie not to tell her mom about the surprise party she was planning for her. It was a good thing she wasn't staying long.

Roselle walked in with Joan; they were both carrying different paper products. When they walked into the lunchroom they were both surprised at all the food. It was going to be a good night. They went to their table; Marge was sitting at it eating her lunch. Looking around the room everyone was all smiles. They asked Marge if it was good and she told them, "yes it's so good, you have to try the sweet potato pie!" Roselle and Joan both knew they were going to save room for dessert. All day the lunchroom was packed. Even the people in the office participated. It really was the best carry in ever!

Lenny was leaving as Roselle and Joan were talking to Marge. He stopped at their table and told them all to enjoy their supper. In his head he was thinking...especially you Marge. Eat up!

After he left Marge told them that Lenny went down on the elevator with her last night and walked her to her car. They couldn't believe he didn't take the stairway. Marge told them he asked her what she was going to do after retiring. They all thought that was a bunch of bull, he never cared about anyone but himself. They were glad she didn't have to walk to her car alone though. Roselle thought it was odd that he walked Marge to her car, but didn't say anything more about it.

He was full but still had to take Cindy and her mom out to supper. He was going to be busy tomorrow night. When he got there, they were both ready to go. He helped her mom get to the car. They went to dinner and he told them about all the food at the carry in today. Cindy was glad the women were taking care of him. When she was in the office they were always very friendly to her. Roselle was the only one she really knew though because they both volunteered a lot. If it was up to Lenny she wouldn't know any of them. She barely said anything about the women who had died already. She just made sure Lenny was ok because she knew that he made it a point to know all of his people. Cindy was proud of her husband for knowing all his employees names. There weren't many bosses who could or would do that. She was going to be upset in the next couple weeks when something happened to Roselle though. He wasn't going to lose sleep over it; his mind was made up...

# CHAPTER 29

It was finally the day Lenny had been waiting for. He could hardly contain his enthusiasm. He puttered around his house for awhile. He didn't want to get to work too early, knowing he was staying till seven. So he straightened up the house and fiddle farted out in his garage. He took the antifreeze back out there while he was going. Then straightened up the garage too. He figured he might as well mow the lawn before he goes in to work. He had plenty of time. He got the riding mower out and his headphones, and proceeded to get busy. He loved his yard, there was nothing like a fresh mowed lawn. Afterward he took a shower and got ready for work. He didn't go in till after he had lunch too. He couldn't believe he was even hungry, after yesterday! By the time he walked through the lunchroom, it was noon. Everything was cleaned up from the carry in. He hoped Sue didn't have to do it all by herself. That was a lot of food, but I guess everyone took home their own dishes. She would only have to put the paper products in a cabinet they had for stuff like that, and wipe down the tables. The guard would help her put the tables away.

Lenny busied himself with paperwork. He really did miss Bill though. He missed their sports conversations, and generally his company. He hoped Bill missed him too. It was one thing to kill these women, but a whole other thing not to have his best friend. He didn't mind taking these women's best friends though! Oh well, they talk too much anyway, he thought to himself.

He kept looking at his watch, the day just dragged on and on. The human resource lady came in and reminded him they needed to hire some new people to replace women who retired and or passed away. He knew that was coming. She also told him they have plenty of applications. People knew he paid well and took care of his people. When she said that, Lenny thought, oh yeah I take care of them all right. The worst thing about killing these women was, he couldn't brag about it! He could only talk to himself; he didn't even trust Bill enough to tell him. He told her to hire as many as she needed. She said thank you and left his office. He looked at his watch. Great, that took a whole five minutes! He went back to his paperwork and charts and graphs. It was finally five o'clock and Janet popped her head in his doorway and asked if he needed anything before she left. "No Janet I'm fine, have a good night." He decided to play some solitaire on his computer, after she left. He could hardly stand the anticipation. He played till about six, then got up and stretched. He decided to take a walk around the big office where the workers were. He could ask his supervisors how things were going. They liked talking to him. He needed a little man talk anyway. Finally, someone he could talk to about the baseball game from Tuesday night! He talked with them till around six forty five. Then he went back to his office and put his suit jacket on. He double checked that he had the syringes too, Yes they were there. He took a deep breath and went out to the lunchroom where Marge was gathering her things and getting ready to leave.

She said to him "are you walking down with me again Lenny?" With a sneer on his lips he answered her "yes I am, if you don't mind." He knew she would mind later! She answered "no I don't mind the company; I just know you usually take the stairs". Lenny told her "I know, but you're retiring soon and I'm gonna miss some of you high seniority gals". They walked to the elevator and both got in, she pushed the button for the ground floor. They were both parked in the back parking lot. It was a pleasant evening, the sun was still out. He wished it wasn't, because then he would have the cover of darkness. He didn't have a choice; Mother Nature had her own clock. While they were outside, walking to their cars, Lenny reached in his pocket with one hand and took the cap off the syringe. He was ready! There was nobody else in the parking lot but them. He let Marge walk in front of him, while he pretended to enjoy the sunlight. He put the needle in her butt and pushed his concoction through with the plunger. It only took a second. She felt a little pinch but Lenny told her there was a bee on her. She said "hmm it must've stung me as she rubbed her butt cheek a little. Good thing I'm not allergic" Lenny said yeah "I don't think I could handle anything like Mary's death again. "They both shook their heads in agreement on that. He helped her get in her car after being stung by a bee or what she thought was a bee. He said bye and walked to his car. He got in knowing she only had about ten minutes to live. He hoped she got home before anything started happening. He honestly didn't want her crashing her car and hurting someone else. He also thought, my God, it just gets easier and easier.

Marge was driving home and started to not feel good. Her head was pounding so hard, like someone was using a jack hammer on it. She hurried a little because everyone knows you feel better just being in your own home. All the neighborhood kids were on the corners yelling across to each other. She pulled up to her house and parked her car. It was only five minutes from work in good weather and little traffic. She hurried up to get in before any neighborhood kids harassed her. She wasn't in the mood to put up with any of them. As she walked in her house she noticed her chest hurt. She was going to change clothes and started to walk towards her bedroom. She just wanted to get her bra off. It was too tight on her chest. She started to think maybe she's having a heart attack. No, I'm fine I just need to get this bra off and sit down. She got it unhooked and sat down on the chair in her living room. Now her chest was really hurting and she couldn't breathe. It was like someone was sitting on her chest and they wouldn't get off of her. She was sweating like she just finished an aerobic workout. She was having a heart attack. She was terrified because she couldn't move. Her last thought as she closed her eyes knowing the end was near, was how long will it take someone to find me and damn it I never got to retire! She died right there in her chair with her bra on but unhooked! All alone, but with kids on every corner on her street. Nobody knew the woman in the little brick house was dead. Nobody knew the woman in the little brick house had been murdered...

# CHAPTER 30

The next morning, Roselle called Marge to see if she wanted to go with her and Bobbie to the greenhouse on Saturday morning. She didn't get an answer so she left a message on the machine. She told her on the machine that she would talk to her about it at work. Marge had to be at work at eleven. Roselle didn't have to be in till four. When she goes in Marge would be on lunch and they could talk.

Marge never showed up for work. Her supervisor checked to see if she called in to say she was sick or something. Nope, nothing on the call in answering machine. He thought to himself, that's not like Marge. After a couple hours, he decided to call the police department. It wasn't like her to not come in and especially to not call the answering machine to report her excuse. He told the police the circumstances and asked them to do a check on her. She always called in when she wasn't going to come in to work. He knew her neighborhood wasn't real safe too. They said they would go check on her.

When the police got there, her curtains were closed and they couldn't see into the house. The officer knocked on the door to no avail. He then tried turning the door knob to see if it was unlocked. He was surprised that it was. This wasn't a neighborhood where you could just leave your door unlocked. He started to think foul play then, as he opened the door. He and his partner walked in and found Marge slumped over in her chair. Rigor mortis had already reached its peak and was starting to dissipate. They called the coroner and the crime lab because of her neighborhood. The crime team figured her time of death to be around seven fifteen - seven thirty. Nothing was amiss in the house and they decided it was probably a heart attack. She had her bra unhooked too, they figured she must have had some chest pain and was trying to alleviate it. There would be an autopsy though because that was mandatory when you find a dead body under suspicious circumstances. The coroner had her body taken to the morgue. The officers found her address book by the telephone and Marge's son's number and address were listed in the front to call in case of emergency. They wrote his address down and went to tell him the sad news. Her son lived in a much nicer neighborhood. When they told him she had passed away in her home, he was surprised because he thought his mom was in pretty good health. The officers told him they thought it was a heart attack but an autopsy would be performed. They said he could go to the morgue if he wanted to see her before the autopsy. Her son told the officers she was going to retire and next Friday would have been her last day of working. They thought that was awful, you work your whole life looking forward to retiring. They gave him their condolences, he told them thanks and they left.

Her son, Mark, called Roselle and asked her to tell the women at work. Roselle asked him "what happened?" "Well the police think it was a heart attack." Mark answered. "Wow, so many deaths lately" said Roselle." I know, but it's a heart attack, it happens at moms age." "Yeah I guess" said Roselle. She also told him "let me know if you need anything, ok Mark." "Sure Roselle" he answered. They hung up from each other.

Roselle couldn't believe it. Another death, she reminded herself to be extra careful because she wanted to make it to retirement! Too many people weren't making it! She called Joan and told her what happened. They both were dumbfounded. "Her son told me they were doing an autopsy but it looked like a heart attack. That's so sad; I guess she won't be going to Bobbie's friend's greenhouse with us Saturday. She looked fine at work when I saw her at four. I guess that's how heart attacks happen" said Roselle. "yes,without warning! They say heart attacks kill more women because we don't recognize the signs and even if we suspect something we are too quick to dismiss it as heartburn or something." said Joan. Roselle answered her "well I'm going to look up every warning sign there is! Too many of us don't seem to be making it to retirement." She also thought I need to get on that dang bike more too! She knew she could make her heart stronger with exercise.

Lenny was at work when he heard the news. He was actually thrilled it worked and also that she made it home without killing any innocent people. His conscious told him Marge was innocent but he quickly pushed that thought away. He was concerned that the police were the ones to find her. That would mean automatic autopsy. Janet told him Marge's supervisor called the police because she hadn't shown up or called in. It wasn't like her to do that and he was worried. He said she lived in a bad neighborhood too. Lenny knew about her neighborhood but didn't say anything just nodded to Janet and asked her to order flowers. He tried to remember how many people saw him leave with her and walk her to her car. Lenny didn't remember seeing anyone, so he felt he was still the mastermind he was becoming in his head. Nobody pays attention to anyone else these days. They're all oblivious to their surroundings. It was helping him so he didn't mind at all.

Mark and his wife went to the morgue to tell them which funeral home to send the body to when they were finished with the autopsy. The pathologist told them he was sure it was a heart attack, her eyes were closed too so I'm thinking she didn't have a lot of pain. He also told Mark that he had already done a toxicology test and there wasn't anything suspicious in her bloodstream. That wasn't news to Mark; he knew his mom didn't do drugs or even drink alcohol. The fact that they did one was a waste of time and taxpayer money to him. He could've told them they wouldn't find anything unusual. Mark and his wife left there and went to his mom's house to find something pretty for his mom to wear for the funeral. They also went to the funeral home to make arrangements. So much to do, he never imagined he would have to do all this right now. He thought he would be booking a cruise or helping his mom find a house in Florida, anything but this. He was kind of glad the pathologist thought she passed away with very little pain. That was somewhat comforting. She raised him by herself and was all the family he had. He never suspected a thing especially murder...

# CHAPTER 31

Today was Saturday, Roselle and Bobbie were going to her friend Carmel's greenhouse. They both needed to get bulbs to plant this fall for next spring. Bobbie wanted purple tulips and Roselle wasn't sure what she wanted. When they were in the car driving there. Bobbie reiterated that she thought someone was killing her mom's friends! Roselle assured her they were dying and not being killed. She told her "they were just unfortunately all close together. "Bobbie told her "I don't believe that! Something's going on mom!" Roselle said "no, they've done autopsies, everything has come out as accidents or allergies, which we knew about, and Marge's was a heart attack. Nobody's killing anyone" Bobbie answered her "I think that's bullshit, maybe it's the coroner. I don't know, but I'm not buying it. Too many women from the same office! Someone is killing them mom!" Roselle told her "you have got to stop watching all those crime shows on television! They put too many ideas in your head. Quit being ridiculous, they are all just unfortunate deaths." In the back of her mind, Roselle thought about Lenny walking Marge to her car earlier in the week. She didn't tell Bobbie though, because she would've jumped right on that and accused Lenny of being the killer!

Bobbie shut up about it, but she still thought it was too coincidental and couldn't believe her mom didn't see it. They got to the greenhouse and started looking around. Bobbie got her purple tulips and Roselle decided on getting the Tiger Lillie's. Carmel gave them a real good deal and they both appreciated it. They told Carmel thanks and put their bulbs in the trunk and left.

Roselle told Bobbie that Marge's funeral visitation was on Monday and they could go together after they left the soup kitchen. Her actual funeral service would be Tuesday morning. It seemed like that's all she did anymore was go to funerals. She had worn her black dress more in the last two months than she had her entire life! Part of her wanted to agree with Bobbie, but she knew the facts from the autopsies were true. She didn't like it anymore than Bobbie, but there wasn't anything she could do. She only had three weeks till she was out of there. Bobbie dropped her off at home but went in to search to make sure no one was in her house before she went home. Roselle thought Bobbie needed to watch other kinds of television shows, but was glad her daughter cared enough to search her house. I don't know what Bobbie thought she would do if someone would've been in her house. She was shorter than Roselle, and didn't have a gun or anything. Bobbie thought she was a bad ass though, and Roselle let her think that too. Half the battle is in your own mind. If you think you're tough, you will be tough. If you think you're weak, you will be weak. Crap! I forgot my bulbs she said to Sara lee's ashes.

Lenny only had one more person to kill and he would

be finished. He couldn't wait for that day. The last one was going to be the hardest. He even felt bad about it, but not bad enough to use his own money. This was too easy to use his own money plus Cindy would know if there was four hundred thousand dollars missing from their savings. He was a little concerned about Roselle having a dog. He decided he would just take a nice juicy steak with him. There wasn't a dog around that would pass up fresh meat, as long as it's not my meat he thought with a smile. He knew her better than he had any of the others, he also knew she kept herself busy volunteering. That's how Cindy knew her too. She wasn't too upset about any of the other deaths around here, but this one would affect her. This is the one he was dreading. Everyone loved Roselle; she was such a free spirit. This was going to take a little more planning. That was okay, he had three weeks. With Marge just having her heart attack, he needed to wait awhile anyway. Hell, her funeral wasn't till next Tuesday. He needed that to be over with first. He was glad Roselle lived in a safer neighborhood too, for his sake and hers. He was going to have to look up her exact address, memorize it, and drive by it a couple times. She worked the four to midnight shifts, so he could drive by it anytime after work.

Marge's son Mark came in to clean out her locker. The guard was there to let him in and also walked with him upstairs. Roselle and Joan were on break when they walked through the lunchroom. The women both gave him a hug and their condolences and talked for awhile. Everyone was upset that she never got to retire. Mark also told them the coroner ruled it a heart attack. That news didn't surprise anyone, because of the way the police found her. They all wished she would have called an ambulance at the first sign of pain. You never know what people will do though. She probably thought she just needed to get in more comfortable clothes and relax. Lenny came out of his office too, when he heard her son was there. Lenny shook Marks hand and told him how sorry he was about his moms passing. He never said a word about walking out with her that day; Lenny figured if nobody asked, he wasn't volunteering any information. Mark understood and told him thank you. He said "mom will get to enjoy her retirement with Jesus himself." "Yes she will" said Lenny. Knowing full well he killed her! He was getting really good at faking sincerity. No one ever suspected a thing!

Mark cleaned his mom's locker out. The guard helped him carry all her things to his car. They had three boxes full. He was surprised she had so much crap there. Crackers, peanut butter, books, sweaters, all kinds of things. He didn't have a clue what he was even going to do with all of it. He would probably end up giving it to charity after he cleaned out her house and put it up for sale. He knew the house most likely wouldn't sell for a whole lot of money. He was going to be happy just to get it sold!

# CHAPTER 32

Cindy's dad came home late Saturday. She was glad to see him because she was ready to go home and be with her husband. He had caught a lot of fish and had a great time with his buddies. He also had a ton of pink salmon in his cooler. Of course he sent some home with Cindy for her and Lenny. He told her they could smoke them or just bake them or cook them however they liked. He gave them about twenty pounds of fish. Cindy said "wow dad, you filleted them already too. Thanks." "No problem kiddo" said her dad. "This year they had a fish table outside the cabin for cleaning your fish. It was nice not having the cabin kitchen smell so fishy. We had a lot of time in the evenings and we were outside anyway. They fit in the freezer better too." "Well thanks dad I know Lenny will appreciate not having to filet them. I'm going to wait till morning to go home though, so I'm going to put them in the freezer for now. Mom is upstairs in bed already. She's doing really well with her ankle. I think it's much better. She's still having a little trouble with steps sometimes though. Keep an eye on her dad; she still tries to do everything." Cindy said with a smile. "I'm going to bed too, night dad. I love you."

"Good night Cindy and thanks for staying with mom so I could go fishing with the guys. You know I haven't missed one of these trips in fifty years. Part of me thinks mom messed her ankle up on purpose to try to get me to stay home or to get to spend the week with you. Ha-ha, good night honey." Said her dad. Cindy went on upstairs to her old bedroom where she had slept all week. She noticed that she should probably clean her room before she left. It was nice to spend the week with her mom. She actually enjoyed it as an adult. When she was a teen, they argued all the time. Sometimes she really missed not having any kids. She and Lenny had tried but it wasn't meant to be. They even tried in-vitro insemination too, nothing worked. They thought about adoption but never really finished that conversation. Time wore on and now it was too late. Instead they concentrated on themselves. He had to work different hours all the time, and she truly enjoyed her volunteer time. She volunteered at the hospital with the pediatric ward. She got to be around kids that way and it seemed to be enough. She was really tired and fell asleep thinking about the kids she volunteered with.

Lenny couldn't wait for Cindy to get home. He missed her so much, more at the end of the week. He was busy at the beginning of the week. She didn't have a clue that she was living with and loved a murderer. He only had one more, then he would be finished and his life could get back to normal. He knew even as good as he had gotten with killing people; he was finished with it after Roselle. He was actually pretty proud of himself for getting the money back into the executive pension fund. He thought it would be harder moving it around but it turned out to be very simple. Just a matter of transferring funds. No one even batted an eye. Now his thoughts were on Roselle and how he was going to plan that murder out. Cindy would be home, but she had been home when he killed Janice and never knew he had even left the house. He knew Roselle lived too far from work to kill her like he did Marge. She would crash her car for sure and probably kill someone else too. He was thinking he could fake car trouble in her neighborhood, or just sneak in somehow. He remembered the dog bones that fell out of her pocket and reminded himself to get that nice big steak before he went there. He didn't want to get this far in his plan and get caught because of a stupid dog! He only had a couple weeks. Roselle's last week at Coble communications was coming up fast. He wanted to be finished by then.

Bill would be back on Monday. He had been on vacation all week in Florida where his parents relocated after they retired. Hopefully he would be willing to let bygones be bygones. Lenny missed his friend and wanted their old friendship back. He wanted Bill to quit looking at him like he was the devil. Bill suspected Lenny had something to do with the murders but he couldn't prove a thing! All the murders had been perfect. They weren't suspicious or anything. He was pretty proud of that fact. Marge's autopsy had come back with a ruling of heart attack. That's the only one he was really worried about. Everything seemed to work in his favor. It made him feel like a mastermind. The women at work were mystified. They couldn't believe so many of their friends had passed away so close together. They never suspected murder, they didn't know what to suspect. Roselle and Joan whispered a lot to each other. They realized they were the only ones left of their little clique. Pretty soon it would just be Joan but they didn't know that...

# CHAPTER 33

Bill got off the airplane and was glad to be home. He had to work tomorrow and was a little happy about it. He missed his girls from human resource. This vacation he went by himself, no date. He had visited his parents in Naples Florida. It was so hot there; it felt good to be back in the Indiana coolness of fall. His parents were glad he came to see them and showed him off to all of their new friends. Holy cow, how many unmarried daughters could these people have, he thought to himself. So many of his parent's friend's wanted him to meet their daughters. He met a couple of them, just because their parents brought them along to dinner. How convenient he thought, he really didn't mind. It was nice having a pretty girl his own age at the dinner table. Overall it was a nice visit .They bought this condo for winters, but decided to go up early this first year. He wanted to talk to his dad about some of the things Lenny and he had been talking about. He also wanted to tell him about all the deaths, but he couldn't prove anything. His dad probably would have told him, Lenny could never kill anyone. Bill thought he could though; his dad hasn't seen him in a while and didn't know what a greedy bastard he'd turned into. They did always like Lenny though and appreciated that his parents helped Bill with college tuition. They would never think anything bad of him. He thought badly of him, but like he said, he couldn't prove anything! He felt like, what if the deaths were all coincidences? Was he willing to lose a friend he's had for forty years over this? He didn't know the answer to those questions. For now, he decided to mend the friendship but wasn't sure if he was going to trust Lenny ever again. What was the saying? Keep your friends close and your enemies closer. That was going to be his new motto. He didn't want to believe that his best friend was capable of murder. He knew Lenny was capable of being a jerk, but a murderer? That was a whole other thing! He was going to keep an eye on him.

Cindy was coming home today, Lenny could hardly wait. He missed having her home. He missed her cooking and cleaning and all the love she had in her heart for him. He missed having someone who loved him unconditionally. His own hatred of himself was worse when he was alone. When she was home, he didn't think about it so much. She took his mind off a lot of things. He watched her pull into the driveway and put the car into the garage. When she walked in the door he gave her a big kiss. "Man I missed you" he said to her as he gave her a big bear hug. She told him "I missed you too, but I did enjoy the time with my mom." As she hugged him back. She almost forgot to tell him about the salmon filets her dad had sent with her. That would've been disastrous. He went to the garage and got the cooler out of her car. "Wow, that's a lot of salmon" he told her.

"I know! Dad filleted it for us too" Lenny answered her "that's cool, let's have some tonight. I'll cook it on the grill"

Cindy told him "that sounds good to me, I'll make us a salad to go with it." She opened the fridge and noticed there wasn't anything for a salad in it. She told Lenny "looks like I'm going to have to run to the store. What did you eat all week?" "Oh I had fast food most of the time. That's why salmon on the grill and a salad sounds really good" he told her with a big smile on his face. "okay baby, let's get your stomach back to normal" Cindy told him as she was getting ready to go to the store.

Roselle called Bobbie and told her she left her bulbs in the trunk of her car. She had to leave a message on the answering machine, because nobody answered the phone. She decided to ride her bike for her ten minutes. The bike rides had already made a difference in how strong her legs felt. No one else had noticed any changes, but she could feel it. She would ride as fast as she could for as long as she could. She did generally only get her ten minutes, but it was working. She had gotten her time on the bike done every day since she told herself to make it a daily habit. She would watch her wrestling tapes while she rode it. She would get so worked up sometimes that it helped her to pedal faster. Valerie came over when she finished riding her bike. She just lived a block away, and would walk down and visit whenever she got the chance. Right now she was canning tomatoes and came to see if her mom had any jars she wasn't using. Roselle canned fruits and vegetables every year when her daughters were younger. She didn't do it anymore though. She'd decided it was too much work just for one person. Roselle told Valerie to go out to the garage and look for old jars. If she had any, that's where they would be. While Val was in the garage she found old school papers and some of the books they had growing up.

She also found a lot of their old report cards. There was tons of stuff from when her and her sisters were little girls. She sat in the garage for a couple hours just going through stuff. She also found a couple dozen jars. She went in the house and told her mom she was going to go home and get her car. She couldn't carry the stuff she wanted to take. "That's fine, take whatever you want from out there" Roselle told her. When she came back she had Dale with her and he helped her load the car. Roselle went out in the yard and watered her flowers while they were there. Valerie had a nice big garden full of flowers and vegetables. She would send the boys down with fresh veggies all the time. That was nice; Roselle always had a garden before too. When the girls were real small, Roselle had to steal from a neighbor's garden. She had to feed her kids! She promised God that she would have a garden when she could, for any other moms who needed a little help feeding their kids. The girls worked in it all summer. They all knew how to take care of a garden now too. Bobbie didn't have room for a garden because they had a big above ground pool in their yard. Emily probably would have a garden whenever her house was finished being built. If it ever got finished!

Today was Roselle's day off and she just enjoyed puttering around the house and yard. After Valerie and Dale left, she got her book and sat in her chair out on the enclosed porch and read. She loved this porch. She had a comfy reading chair out there and used the sunlight as her lamp. When it got too dark to read she went inside. She was going to love being able to do this every night after she retired. Life would be so easy then. She had so many books she wanted to read!

# CHAPTER 34

Lenny was at his desk looking up files when Bill knocked on his door jamb. "it's open come on in" he told Bill. "How was the vacation?" Lenny asked. "It was great! I went to Naples and visited mom and dad" Bill answered. "How are they doing?" Lenny asked. He was genuinely interested. He did miss Bills parents, but was glad they were able to buy a condo in Florida for retirement. They deserved to be happy. So did all the women you killed he thought. He pushed that thought right out of his head. His conscience would never shut up and let him forget about the murders. Bill said "I heard about Marge. That whole group of women is dwindling down." Lenny told him "I know, Marge had a heart attack, she was in her sixties and obviously didn't take care of herself." "Her viewing is later this morning; I'm going to make an appearance for a short while. Then I have work to do, so I'll be back in the office. Do you mind holding down the fort while I'm gone?" He asked Bill. Bill told him "sure no problem". Lenny knew there was no way he was going to tell him he killed her but he wanted to brag so badly! He was so proud of himself for going to the library and researching how to kill her. He hated that he had to keep it to himself. When he first approached Bill about all of it, he thought he could trust him. Bill had proven to him that he couldn't though. He actually did trust that Bill wouldn't tell anyone, but he wanted someone he could talk to about all of it. That really saddened him. He really wanted to tell him how clever he had been. Gheese what was wrong with him! He didn't know. He knew it was wrong, but he still wanted to brag so badly!!

Bill wouldn't pat him on the back and say good job, he would probably freak out and tell the police. Lenny could never let him know about the murders!

Bill told Lenny about all his parents' friends daughters. Lenny told him "you need to pick one of these ladies and settle down. I think you would love married life". "Ha! I don't think so" Bill said. He liked having different girls for different situations. "Dad told me to tell you hello for him. I better get back to my office and catch up on everything I missed" Bill told him." "Okay come on back when you get caught up and want to talk." Lenny answered him. The conversation was a little strained and tense but Lenny was glad Bill came into his office. He thought maybe they could get their friendship back to where it was before the mess Lenny created started.

Bobbie called Emily and asked about the piñata. Emily told her it was already started and should be finished in plenty of time. Bobbie said the cake was ordered too and would be delicious. Everything is falling into place. "I'm so excited for mom! It's going to be hard not telling her about it while we're at the soup kitchen and Marge's viewing today." Bobbie asked Emily "are you going to the viewing too?" Emily said "no, but I am planning on going to the funeral tomorrow." "Ok I'll see you there. I'm going to pick Val and mom up and we're all going to ride together." Emily said "I might be late, save me a seat by you guys, ok?" "Ok bye, love you" said Bobbie.

Roselle and Bobbie rode together to the soup kitchen. Roselle knew how Bobbie felt about all the funerals the two of them had gone to lately. It really was a coincidence though. They went and made the soup and did their regular stuff for the soup kitchen. It felt like they were just going through the motions. Everyone at the kitchen knew, another friend of Roselle's had passed away. They all gave her their condolences. It was so sad. How many funerals could a person go to before they started thinking about their own mortality? Bobbie and Roselle left the soup kitchen and went straight to Marge's viewing. There were quite a few of the women from Roselle's work there. They all sat together and talked quietly amongst themselves. Lenny walked in and talked to Mark and his wife. He gave them his condolences, and then walked over to where Roselle and her daughter were with the other women. They talked for a little while then Lenny left. He fought the urge to tell Roselle you're next! He was thinking it though, good thing she couldn't read minds he thought to himself. After he left, the women were saying how thoughtful it was that Lenny came today. If they only knew... He was the one who caused this funeral to even happen, they wouldn't be so proud of him. The brown nosers especially liked it, now they had something else to talk to Lenny about at work. Roselle and Bobbie stayed all afternoon. There were just too many of their friends coming in and out. Marge had been a good friend to the whole family and deserved their time. That's all they could give her now. Nothing else mattered. They felt bad for Mark and his family.

On the way home, Roselle told Bobbie "when I die, I want to be buried in a fringe dress." "Seriously mom?" Bobbie asked. "Yes it's going to be a party when I meet Jesus and I want to be dressed appropriately!" Said Roselle. "Wow mom, who knew? That's the last thing I would've thought you would want to wear when you meet Jesus" exclaimed Bobbie. "you're not dying though mom! If you die, I know something's going on then! I still think someone's killing your little group of friends!" Bobbie told her mom. "Whatever" said Roselle.

She didn't believe it. She couldn't believe it! If they were, she was probably next! Yikes, she couldn't have thoughts like that in her head! She would be so pissed if she died now, before she got to live her lifelong dream of retiring. She was mad that her friends didn't get to retire. She was going to do whatever it took to get to her retirement day!

# CHAPTER 35

Marge's funeral just started when Emily sat down with her mom and sisters. She whispered, "Sorry" to them. The funeral home was pretty full but there were still seats available. It was a short service then everyone went to the cemetery for the burial service. It was a cool fall day. Everyone was wearing jackets and wishing the sun would come out. After the service everyone just walked from group to group to talk.

Lenny had Roselle's address and planned on driving by it after work today. He could tell by the address it was in a very safe neighborhood. He was glad to see that! Marge's had been a disaster waiting to happen. He felt lucky that he hadn't got shot when he was in her neighborhood. He didn't need to go all the way into it to see the danger. It was plain to see. There were so many damn kids on the corners. He truly hoped Sue would get out of that area too. That murder was over now though. Lenny had to admit it was a success! He wasn't sure about the plan for Roselle. He would know more once he drove past her house tonight. He didn't know how close her neighbors were or if she had a door he would be able to get in without being seen. He still didn't even know how he was going to kill her. He had homework to do on this murder. She came in at four so he could leave anytime after that. During the day today he had mostly low seniority employees working. A lot of the women were at Marge's funeral. He could hardly hold it against them since he killed her. It was his fault they were all gone right now. Bill even came in and said it was eerily quiet in the big office where all the workers worked. Lenny soberly reminded him the regular women were at Marge's funeral. "Oh that's right, how was the visitation yesterday? I never got a chance to come back over here" said Bill. "It was fine, I met Roselle's daughter. She looks a lot like her mom, only lots younger. Her voice sounds the same as hers too" answered Lenny. "That's funny isn't it? Do you think either one of us sound like our parents?" Asked Bill. Lenny laughed and said "I don't think so but it's hard to tell when you're not side by side. Maybe that's why it was so obvious." Lenny finished the conversation by telling Bill "the normal people would be in for the night shift."

After the funeral, Roselle and Bobbie made plans to go to Josh's football game on Friday. High school games were so much fun when your grandson was the starting left tackle thought Roselle. Bobbie told her mom "let's get together before then and get our bulbs planted." "Hmm, how about Thursday morning? It's supposed to be nice that day." Said Roselle. "Sure that sounds good" said Bobbie. Emily and Valerie just looked at each other. Emily asked "why do you two always plan stuff when we can't come?" Valerie added "yeah you know we have to work during the day!" Bobbie just told them "wa, wa, wa crybabies Emily you could come, you're just sewing! Val, I'm sorry but we both work in the evening." At that Emily punched Bobbie in the Arm and

Roselle had to tell her to knock it off! "my goodness you guys, we're still at a funeral, behave!" said Roselle Emily looked around and then said "no one saw me punch Bobbie! It's okay" Roselle said "I saw it!" If you guys want to come and help us plant bulbs then by all means come on over!" Bobbie just smirked at Emily while she rubbed her arm. Roselle told them she had to work that night and asked Valerie and Bobbie if they were ready to go. "Yes I am" said Bobbie. Valerie agreed with Bobbie. They all told Emily goodbye and did a group hug before they separated. Roselle and Valerie rode with Bobbie. She needed to drop them both off then get home and get herself ready for work. She told Roselle that she should stop at the sandwich shop and get something healthy for her supper. Bobbie worked in a retail store and had to go in earlier than normal to replenish the school shoe stock. Tj was going to have to cook tonight. He would probably make breakfast food. The kids didn't mind, they loved when dad cooked breakfast, even if it was for supper. They didn't like anything else he cooked. Bobbie didn't either, he wasn't the best cook unless it was breakfast or hot dogs and macaroni and cheese. That was his repertoire, she thought with a smile. Valerie told Bobbie and Roselle "you guys can plant some bulbs at my house if you want." Bobbie answered her "we'll see if we have any left, if we do, we just might." "That would be cool" said Valerie.

Valerie's garden was amazing; strangers would stop when she was outside to ask if they could walk through it. She had a perfect combination of fruits, and vegetables, and flowers. She even had grape vines, and would make her own grape jelly with her grapes. She had an old wheelbarrow in her yard that she had purple petunias planted in. She also had a trellis with her morning glories blooming every morning in her yard. Bobbie's favorite was her moonflower. It was gorgeous. She had to go in the evening to see it bloom, but it was truly worth it. What a beautiful flower! If they did plant some tiger Lillie's at Val's, she wasn't sure where to put them. Valerie's yard was so organized. She wasn't sure she wanted to mess her yard up with random tiger Lillie's.

# CHAPTER 36

Roselle stopped and bought a sandwich for supper on her way to work. She would have liked to go to the dinner Marge's family had put together after her burial. She had to work though, some of the other women there had to go in tonight too. When she got to work and went into the lunchroom, she noticed the mood was pretty somber. That's to be expected she thought. Funerals and death were hard on everyone. The better you know someone, the worse you feel when they die. All the women here were a tight knit group. Oh sure you had your cliques, everyone had their own friends. As a whole group though, they all knew each other. There were only two hundred or so workers here. All women and mostly divorced women. Trying to pay their bills and take care of their families. They've had a lot of deaths lately. It was starting to effect morale.

Lenny walked through the lunchroom while Roselle and Joan were sitting at the "retiree table". Roselle was telling Joan that Bobbie thinks someone is killing the women there. Joan told her "I wonder too!" They talked quietly to each other as they watched Lenny come through. They both said to each other, he looks happy. Roselle even asked him "what are you so happy about Lenny?" He told them "Cindy has been gone for a week helping her mom and was finally home." Joan said while smiling "she was gone for a whole week. Wow and you survived! Good job". Lenny said "yes, her mom sprained her ankle and her dad had a fishing trip. She went to help her out. I really missed her too." He was thinking, you're not going to survive much longer though Roselle. Enjoy the time you have! Roselle told him she had broke her ankle a couple years ago and her daughter helped her out too. She didn't need to stay there though because she only lived about ten minutes from her. Lenny made a mental note - daughter ten minutes away. Roselle and Joan stood up from their seats; they both patted him on the back and said "good for you!" We're glad she's home too." Then they walked into the office. Roselle was thinking, and life goes on. No matter how bad you felt about someone's death. The sun was going to rise the next morning. It brought a new meaning to life. Enjoy it while you can because it doesn't last forever. When her older brother died from cancer, she was so depressed. They were very close, it put her into such a funk she wasn't sure she would or even could come out of it. Her friends helped her through it by keeping her involved in everything that was going on around her. The soup kitchen helped too because it taught her to appreciate what she had. There were so many people who didn't have anything. You have to love the life you're in or change it, either way it's up to you as an individual.

Lenny shut his computer down and walked out with Janet. He was headed to Roselle's neighborhood. It was still daylight so he had to be careful. She lived in the next town.

School had started but there would probably be kids outside playing. Maybe I'll get lucky and they'll all be inside doing homework. The days were getting shorter and shorter. The sunset was still around nine o'clock. Tonight he was just going to do a drive by, not too intense.

He finally got to her neighborhood; there were kids outside on their bikes. He found her house, it was on a corner. It looked to him like she probably used her side door. She had a nice enclosed patio on that side. It looked like she used the patio a lot. Her newspaper was still lying on a table she had by her chair. The house was closer to the road than he was used to. He went around the block again. She had a patio by the back door too. He decided he was going to have to come back after dark because the kids on bikes were watching him too much. Damn kids!

What he didn't know was one of the kids watching him was Dale. This was his grandma's house and he wondered why this guy was looking at her house so much and driving so slow! He and his friends stayed close especially when they saw him come around the block again! Dale didn't recognize him, but thought maybe he was a salesman or something. When he went home for supper, he didn't tell his mom because he actually forgot about it. Valerie didn't ask either because she was still busy canning tomatoes. She didn't know to ask. She didn't see Lenny circle the block twice. Dale and his friends got to playing and riding around the neighborhood. He just forgot about it. He was only ten; he didn't know this was the guy who was going try to murder his grandma...

# CHAPTER 37

It was Thursday morning. Bobbie and Roselle were going to plant their bulbs today. It was going to be a nice day, the sun was already shining. Bobbie didn't want to go to her moms too early because she worked till midnight. She made herself a cup of tea and a piece of toast with orange marmalade. The kids had just left for school. She had an idea where her mom was going to want to plant her tiger Lillie's. What she really needed to do was figure out where she wanted her tulips. She took her cup of tea and went outside to walk around the house. She really wanted them out front but every time she planted flowers there Tj ended up mowing them down! They would be so pretty out front along the porch! She was going to plant them there and tell Tj to let them grow! They were a spring flower; he would still be able to use the weed wacker after they died out. Dang it, if she could get him to leave it alone, she could plant some annuals out front too. She would love to plant some gerbera daisies there! That's what she really wanted, she thought with a smile. Both her sisters had lots of pretty flowers. Why did she have to be the one to marry the guy who liked uncluttered yards? He did a great job with the grass; it was the plushest on their block. It actually looked like a carpet. She thought it would be even nicer with some colorful flowers decorating it. The back yard was out of the question for flowers because the pool was back there and when you have a pool you have lots of kids. They trampled everything plus grunt thought the backyard was his. They had a park right behind their house but in the park you had to have your dogs on a leash. Grunt liked to be free, so yeah the back yard was his. It was fenced with a nice wooden privacy fence. He loved it out there. She fed him, and then went to get changed to go to her moms. Finally ready, she put his leash on and took him with her. Bobbie grabbed a shovel out of their shed too because she didn't think her mom had two, and she didn't want to have to do all the digging. Mom loved grunt and he loved her. Mom's yard was fenced in too. It was chain-link which grunt liked better. He could see the squirrels better! He loved riding in the car too! All you had to say was "come on grunt, let's go bye bye" and he was ready to go!

They arrived at Roselle's around nine thirty. She was up and out on her enclosed porch reading the paper. "Good morning mom, I hope you don't mind I brought grunt with me". "No I don't mind, we're going to be outside anyway. Here boy," Roselle said as she went in the house and got him a peanut butter bone. Bobbie asked "where were you thinking of planting the tiger Lillie's?" "Well I was thinking out front by the door, close to the house. We can put them about a foot away and they'll fill out on their own. Tiger Lillie's multiply fast!" Answered Roselle. "hmmm that's where I was thinking too" said Bobbie. Roselle asked Bobbie "did you bring your shovel? I only have one" "yes I did "Bobbie told her as she was going to her car to get it. Roselle thought dang it; she was going to have to shovel too. Bobbie was the only one of her kids who still treated her like a capable adult. Sometimes she liked it other times she didn't. They were laughing about Tj mowing her flowers and how he probably wasn't going to like that she was planting more! Bobbie said he would get over it because she had news for him; she was planting some in their yard too! They both thought that was funny. The two of them got busy digging up the dirt and planting the bulbs and weren't paying any attention to the cars going by them. If they had been, they would have seen Lenny drive by the house! Grunt chased his car to the corner but he was used to traffic going by his own house, so he went back to what he was doing. He was busy watching the squirrels back by the garage. He was standing real still trying to fool them into thinking he was a statue so they would come into the yard and he could chase them. The squirrels weren't fooled though and stayed where they were safe, on the other side of the fence. Neither Bobbie nor Roselle paid any attention to grunt barking at any cars going by. They were busy digging to plant soon to be flowers.

Lenny drove past Roselle's house on his way to work. Shit! She was out in her yard with her daughter. They were digging in the front yard. He saw the dog too. It kind of looked like a bear. It had long black hair, and looked like a Labrador mix. Shit! It was racing him to the corner. All he could think was... Don't look up Roselle, don't look up! He reminded himself to bring the steak when he comes back. When he saw them in the yard he wanted to duck down in his seat. He didn't though because it wouldn't have been safe. They were both digging and talking. He could see their lips moving. They weren't paying attention to anything but their shovels and their conversation. Thank goodness because Roselle knew where he lived and that her house was out of the way for him to be going to work. She would know he had no business being in her neighborhood. They must be getting ready to plant something. He was thinking have your fun all you want right now... Your days are numbered. It didn't matter to him though because he knew Roselle wasn't going to live long enough to see whatever they were planting bloom.

# CHAPTER 38

When they finished planting the tiger Lillie bulbs at Roselle's, Bobbie went on home. Grunt didn't want to leave his grandma's house because he loved watching the cars drive by. He saw Lenny drive by and chased him from one end of the yard to the other end. He was the only one that saw him though. Bobbie got him in the car and threw her shovel in the trunk of the car. "Ok mom, I'll see you later. Stop by and get some supper on your way to work." "Ok and thanks for helping me with those flowers. We didn't have any left to plant in Val's yard but oh well" said Roselle. "Yeah, I know. I didn't want to mess her yard up anyway. Love ya mom bye" said Bobbie. "Carry on" said Roselle.

Bobbie was thinking, man my shoulders and my back hurt from that shoveling. Mom's probably going to be sore too. I'm glad I did most of the shoveling. Ugh, but now I have to do my own flowers.

She got home and put grunt in the back yard because it was too nice of a day for him to be indoors. Then she went into the house and put shorts on. The sun was out and she liked having a nice tan. Anytime she could get her summer tan to last longer, she would do it. She and Tj lived on a busy street. There were always cars going by out front. They had a swing on their porch that they agreed was the best thing they ever bought for the house. Many a night was spent on that porch swing, watching traffic go by, snuggled up to each other. Grunt would have to be on the leash out front because it wasn't fenced like in the back yard. He liked watching the cars too, but he couldn't chase them like at his grandma's house. They also would sit and watch the kid's race up and down the block. As parents, you had to do something to burn that energy off of them. Sometimes they had all the neighborhood kids racing each other. Tj would get his stopwatch out and time them. The kids loved being timed, and would race for hours. Anything to get them to sleep at night! Those were the good old days. Now the kids were older and into more sports. Josh with his football and Liddy in softball.

Bobbie poured herself some lemonade and got some chicken out of the freezer for supper. Then she went out on the swing. After she finished her lemonade, she got started on her own flowers. She wanted to plant them in a circle and put a smiley face in it. Then thought better and put them in rows. By the time she was finished Michael was getting home from school, the other two were in sports and got home later. Bobbie decided to bake the chicken and have a squash and zucchini recipe she loved. She also made rice cooked in chicken broth with a little of the squashes in it for supper. Michael had to work tonight so he said he'd eat there. He didn't like zucchini anyway. He worked in the kitchen of a private club. They were teaching him how to do some of the cooking at work. Michael thought about being a chef since he learned to make a couple impressive dishes. He almost burned the house down though when him and a friend made bananas foster one night. Bobbie had to tell him he could only cook when she or dad was home. They were proud that he was interested in something as cool as being a chef. It was good to broaden your horizons. Michael just wanted to impress girls with his flambé cooking skills. "Ok, more zucchini for us. You can eat there, grandmas stopping by in a little bit for some supper; she would love to see you" Said Bobbie. Michael told her "I can't mom, I have to be there at three thirty to help the sous-chef." "Wow, you better get a move on then!" said Bobbie. "ok love ya" said Michael as he headed back out the door. "love you too" said Bobbie, but he was already gone and probably didn't hear her. Sometime it was hard to have these babies, then they grow up. You have to learn how to let them go. It doesn't just happen all of a sudden one day. When she thought about it, in less than five years it would be just her and Tj. Wow! It will be nice to go out to dinner without spending a small fortune. She thought. She would miss them but you have to let them go. They have to learn just like we did, that you can survive on your own. You make do with what you have.

Tj was walking in the back door with grunt hot on his trail. The two of them were quite the pair! Tj was a runner and grunt liked to go with him too. Only if it wasn't raining. When it would rain grunt would see Tj tying his running shoes and fake that he had a limp. So Tj would leave him at home. When Tj got back home grunt was fine. When it was nice out and Tj would tie his shoes, grunt would immediately go into stretch mode. He was a smart dog! He didn't like to get wet but he was smart enough to get out of it. Together, they were best friends. Grunt had the most personality of any dog Bobbie and Tj ever had in their whole lives.

Bobbie told him "supper would be ready soon. Hey I planted some spring flowers out front today too" Tj said "crap you know I hate mowing around that stuff! Just don't plant as many flowers as your mom has please." Bobbie told him "I know, but they're spring flowers, they die out quick. It will be fine, you'll see" She wasn't going to tell him about the annuals she wanted to plant just yet. "Go take your shower, by then supper will be done. Mom might be here too so wear a towel!" "Ok cool" he answered. He loved Roselle. "Supper smells good too by the way" he added as he gave her a kiss and went to the bathroom to shower. Bobbie decided to let her mom tell him about the flowers they planted at her house, she wasn't going anywhere near that!

Roselle stopped by on her way to work and Bobbie had a plate all ready for her to take. "Yum this smells really good, Bobbie" said Roselle. "Thanks mom, I think you'll like it" Roselle dug a peanut butter bone out of her pocket for grunt who was waiting patiently for it." you're such a good boy grunter" she said to him. Tj came out of the bathroom in his towel and said "hey Rose, what's up? You know college football has started. Are you going to watch the game here on Saturday?" Roselle told him "I'm going to Josh's game tomorrow night, that might be enough football for me but we'll see. What are you cooking?" She laughed. Tj told her "I'm not sure, maybe some brats on the grill. Chips too probably" Roselle told him "if I come I'll bring some of my horseradish dip." "Sounds good to me" he said. "thanks for supper you guys .. Carry on" said Roselle as she walked out the door and went on her way to work. It had already been a long day. Grunt watched her leave out the front door with his head cocked to one side, like he was thinking.. Stay grandma, I know you have more bones in your pocket and I didn't even get to sit on your lap yet.

He got over her leaving as soon as she was gone and went to see what Tj was doing.

# CHAPTER 39

Lenny couldn't believe he just about blew it yesterday. Driving past Roselle's house on the way to work was careless. All it would have taken is for either one of them to be looking his way when he drove by. He had met Roselle's daughter at Marge's visitation earlier this week. He knew she would have recognized him if she saw him. Another reason he felt a higher power was helping him. Everything always seemed to work out. Today was Friday, he only had another week to fulfill his plan. He didn't want to do it her last week of work. He wanted to be done with this whole mess by next Friday. That was the deadline in his head. He knew it was going to be after midnight when he did it. So that meant he was going to have to drug Cindy again. She liked having a glass of wine with supper so that wouldn't be too hard. He would have some with her too. Whenever he drank with her, she drank more than normal. He really needed to figure out how he was going to pull this one off. He'd been so lucky so far. Could he still be lucky, just one more time? This was going to be harder too, because he knew Roselle so well. He wasn't sure if he could stand listening to the women in the office talk about her death. They wouldn't get over this one so easily. They all loved her. The other women he killed were liked too, but none of them were as personable as Roselle. She knew everyone's name just like Lenny. He was going to do it though. This would be the last one, and then he could get back to normal. Normal ? He asked himself. What was normal anymore? His conscience told him, not killing anyone was normal! Shut up conscience he thought. That was a problem he thought about too. Would he be able to keep this to himself forever? If his conscience wouldn't shut up now, would it ever shut up? He really wanted to tell someone, anyone how clever he was!

Today was Roselle's day off. She had plans to go to Josh's football game with Bobbie and Tj. Liddy would probably go too. Freshmen girls liked going to the games so they could check out the upper class boys. She would probably have a couple friends with her, so they could walk around together. Mike would probably have to work. She threw a blanket in her car to sit on at the game. Those bleachers were hard on the buns after a while. Bobbie and Tj liked to sit on the fifty yard line. Josh knew that's where they would be and whenever they announced his name for a tackle, he knew right where to look for his parents. Tonight was homecoming, so it was going to be crowded. Josh was on the homecoming court. Who would have ever thought he would have any interest in homecoming? I guess he would, anytime there was a pretty girl, josh was somewhere close. Bobbie told her that josh had girls calling the house at all hours for him. She had to tell him "no incoming calls after nine o'clock, dad had to get up early!" Roselle felt sorry for the girl he would have to walk with. He would be all sweaty and dirty from the game and she would be in a semi formal dress. Oh well, that's how high school always handled homecoming. They couldn't make the boys put a suit on at half time. It was hard enough putting all those pads and spandex pants on! Then, after the game was a homecoming dance.

She was going to go to Bobbie's house early and have supper with them before the game. They would then all ride together in one vehicle. It was going to be hard enough finding a parking spot for one car. There wasn't any sense taking two vehicles. They could stuff Liddy and her friends in wherever they could fit. They were small enough she thought to herself. It should be a fun night. Josh's team only had one loss for the year. Winning the game was always more fun than losing. One of the women Roselle worked with had a son on the team, so she would probably see her there too.

She went out on the enclosed patio and read the paper. She took her whole pot of tea with her too. That way she could stay out there all morning if she wanted to. She could see her mums from the patio. They were yellow and looked very pretty. Yellow mums were Bobbie's idea. They made her think of smiley faces! She's always been kind of goofy thought Roselle.

Bill went into Lenny's office. "Hey, you want to watch the football game at my house tomorrow?" Bill asked. "I don't know, are you going to have a girl over too? If you did, I could bring Cindy and she would have someone to talk to." Lenny told him. Bill said "I guess I could ask Kathy, they got along great at the lake house." "That would be great" said Lenny. "Cindy liked her a lot, she wishes you would marry that one" he said with a big smile. "Well I don't know about all that" said Bill "but I'll see if she can come over. My house one o'clock "he told Lenny. "I'll bring some beer" said Lenny. "Sounds good! I'll see you then" Bill said with a smile. That was nice, finally a conversation like they used to have thought Lenny. He decided he was going to worry about killing Roselle next week. He needed a break! Maybe his conscience would forget about the murders he already did and shut the hell up!

# CHAPTER 40

Today was going to be a football day. Lenny and Cindy stopped and bought some cold beer to take with them to Bills house. Cindy was excited she would get to see Kathy again. They got along great. Secretly she wished Bill and her would get married. Weddings were always fun. She loved getting dressed up and a nice dinner, then dancing. Bill was the same age as Lenny and she wasn't sure he could handle being married this late in life. He was so set in his ways. They were both getting close to fifty years old. They weren't there yet but close enough. She needed to talk to Lenny about when he was thinking of retiring. He probably could be semi retired now. The business belonged to his dad first and he retired and gave it to Lenny. They didn't have any kids so she wasn't sure what options they had for keeping it in the family. They would need to talk about that.

They arrived at Bills house, Lenny put the beer in the fridge. Cindy started helping Kathy with side dishes. Bill was outside cooking on the grill. He had it already going with brats. The girls were working on a salad for all of them. They both liked football, but not like the guys did. They would be glad if the local team won, but if they lost they were fine too. The guys were another story. If they lost the guys would certainly be upset. It's just a stupid game thought Cindy. Why do men get so worked up over a loss?

Roselle called Bobbie to see if they had horseradish in their fridge. They did, so she took the cream cheese and went on over to their house. She grabbed a few peanut butter bones for grunt too. He would never forgive her if she forgot his bones. When she parked out front, she could see him in the glass door wagging his whole butt. Dogs were always so happy to see you! He made her smile. Tj was getting the charcoal lit on the grill. Liddy had a friend over too. She grew up with her dad yelling at the television every Saturday and usually just stayed in her room. Her friend and her would come out when Tj was yelling, just to make fun of him. Josh and Mike were both home to watch the game with their dad too. Everyone on their block would be watching the same game. You could hear the neighbor's yelling and cheering too. Bobbie took the cream cheese from her mom and started making the dip. She grew up eating this dip. She and both her sisters knew how to make it. She didn't have a big white dip bowl like her mom but she had a glass bowl to make it in. Mom always said it tastes better in glass compared to plastic. Bobbie already had homemade macaroni and cheese in the oven too. She had the chips poured in a big bowl and was ready for the dip. The game started in half an hour. Bobbie could finally sit down, since her part of the food was either done or baking. Bobbie went to the living room because she had to get away from the chips and dip. She had no self control when it came to moms dip!

Roselle was telling Bobbie about Emily wanting her to go

on a singles cruise after she retired. Bobbie thought it was a good idea too, but knew her mom would go crazy with that much water around her. It wouldn't be any fun if you're afraid for your life. Roselle wasn't sure about the boyfriend thing. It's been a long time since she's had anyone tell her what to do! Bobbie told her "if he's too bossy... just break up with him. Nobody said you had to stay with him. Get what you want and get out." Roselle said "what do you mean get what I want" they both laughed at that.

Kick- off! Tj told them to be quiet. Bobbie said "what, you can't see, if you can't hear?" She and Roselle laughed then they were quiet till the commercials. Tj was totally serious about his football! He would talk and laugh during time outs and commercials, but when the game was on he was all football! The boys were pretty serious till halftime. Then it was time to eat, and they liked their food. Game food was always the best! During the second half, Roselle went and took a nap on Bobbie and Tj's bed. She had to work tonight, and they lived closer to her work than she did. They had a waterbed, she really liked it. This was the first time she ever slept on a waterbed, she always thought it was for hippies! I might have to get me one of these, Roselle thought. She was asleep within minutes and slept for an hour. Then she got up and went in to work.

Lenny and Bill were pretty serious about their football too. They were inside watching the game while the girls were outside on the porch talking. Cindy was telling Kathy about her volunteer work. She told her the only bad thing was that the kids were so sick sometimes and that was hard to deal with. It was harder on the parents though. She couldn't imagine what they went through. Kathy was a school teacher and taught second grade. She loved the kids and told Cindy, she should come and volunteer in her class. She sounded perfect for her classroom! She told her it was all seven and eight year olds with all their energy and curiosity. She would love to have her help. Cindy thought that sounded great!

While watching the game Lenny thought, maybe he could throw a rock or ball in Roselle's window. She would most likely let the dog out, and he could let it outside the gate. Crap, but then it would probably start barking! He thought well I better take the steak with me. That would keep the dog quiet and busy! He didn't want to get lazy or sloppy on this last one. He needed to check the schedule for the coming week. He would do that on Monday, because he was going to spend his Sunday at home with Cindy, not thinking about Roselle or murder or anything having to do with work! It would be difficult to kill Roselle but she was just one little old lady against him. He could do it. She looked as weak as all the other women he'd already killed. He had to do it!

# CHAPTER 41

Lenny went into work today at nine. It was refreshing to get to work regular daytime hours. He had to check the schedule today, but enjoyed knowing he could leave at five. It was like he was a normal business owner. He was going to drive past Roselle's house again tonight. He was hoping those boys wouldn't be around on their bikes again. It sure would be nice if he could go up to the door. He wanted to look in the windows and see the layout of her house. He knew he couldn't take that chance in broad daylight though. She only had one neighbor that would see him. They had to be older too because there weren't any toys or bikes in their yard. There wasn't really anything in their yard that gave any indication that anyone even lived there! If they were old people, they probably looked out their window every time a car went by he thought. Old people liked spying on their neighbors! It would be the highlight of their day if they saw someone sneaking around Roselle's house. They would probably call the police and report it too! Today he would go around twice but one time, he was going to look at the neighbor's house and see if they were looking at him.

Bill came into his office to rehash the football game from Saturday. They won and that was nice. You never knew with college football. One week they would be good and the next week they would have too many injuries or some other excuse if they lost. Bill and him made plans to watch next Saturdays game at Lenny's house. Bill asked "oh yeah, did Cindy tell you she's going to volunteer in Kathy's classroom?" Lenny told him "yeah she mentioned something about that. She said it might be nice working with kids who weren't sick." Bill told him "yeah I know. I don't think I could work with sick kids. I don't know how she can do that every day. Kathy's classroom might be just what Cindy needs." Lenny said "as long as it doesn't make her want to try to have a baby again. That was so hard on her, I couldn't go through that again. Plus now we're too old to have a baby." Bill said "yes, you are, old man!" with a big grin on his face. They both laughed at that because they knew they were the same age. Bill went back to his office after that remark. Lenny absolutely loved having his old friend back. Bill wasn't even looking at him like he was the devil anymore. It was like Bill forgot about the embezzlement too. He didn't know if Bill was trying to trick him into admitting he killed those women or really was being his friend again. Lenny was so paranoid about everything. Sometimes when he walked through the lunchroom he could see the women watching him. He could see them whispering to each other. Did they know he killed them? Had the outside of him changed as much as the inside of him? He still had the brown nosers up his butt as soon as he walked in the lunchroom, they would never give up on him. It was the other women he worried about, the ones who didn't talk to him. The ones who talked so low he couldn't hear them. Did they know about him, he wondered.

Roselle saw Val's car was still at her house. She thought Val should have been at work. She got dressed and walked down the street to Val's. Roselle knocked on the door because it was locked. She always locked her doors, that's crazy thought Roselle. This was a very safe neighborhood. There was never any trouble or any reason for the police to be in their area. Val answered the door and let her mom inside. Roselle asked her "are you sick?" Val said "not sick sick, just sick of work" she laughed. "I really just want to get those tomatoes finished up" Roselle said "oh ok, I saw your car was still parked on the curb and wanted to make sure everything was ok". Val said "yes I'm fine. Do you want a cup of tea while you're here?" "Sure" answered Roselle. They talked about tomatoes and flowers and Roselle finally getting to retire. At least Valerie didn't go on about all the women who died at her work lately. After she drank a couple cups of tea with Val she went home to her porch and her newspaper. Then she made a pan of brownies to take to work with her tonight.

Roselle's daughters were as happy as she was about her retiring. She had so many plans. She was going to visit her sister, Dolly, in Texas and her brothers in Ohio too. Dolly was thirteen years younger than Roselle. She used to stay with her in the summers once she turned sixteen, and could drive. That was when the girls were younger and she needed the help of a babysitter. Her daughters all loved Dolly too. She was the fun aunt who wasn't afraid to try new things. She would take the girls to the park, and try skateboarding or whatever she just felt like doing. It would be so nice to see her. It had been at least five years since they've seen each other. They talked on the phone a lot but it wasn't the same. Dolly had a garden she was always bragging about too. Her son Chad still lived at home, he was the same age as Roselle's grand kids. She missed her sister and couldn't wait to see her. Roselle wanted to take a trip on the train too. They had all kinds of places you could visit. The Rocky Mountains, Las Vegas, pretty much anywhere you wanted to go. There was a train that could take you there. She also had a whole list of books she wanted to read. She could hardly wait, two more weeks and she would be free! Oh crap Bobbie was here to go to the soup kitchen. Roselle hurriedly closed her door and got in Bobbies car and they went to make and serve soup.

Lenny checked the schedule and saw that Roselle worked every evening except for Wednesday. He was hoping she went to bed early on her day off. He would never know though till that night. It sure would make this easier on him if she was asleep when he snuck in or whatever he decided to do. He didn't really have a plan yet. All he knew was that he had one syringe left and was going to use it that night. If she was asleep, he could just inject her and she would just never wake up. If she was awake, he wasn't sure what he would do. Everyone else had gone so smoothly, he honestly didn't anticipate any problems. He did need to check on those neighbors though. He had the syringe hidden in his desk under a stack of papers. Don't forget that either, he told himself.

It was around three forty five, Lenny decided to take a walk through the lunchroom. The night shift ladies were coming in now. Yum, somebody made brownies and brought them in for everyone. Lenny helped himself to one, the women knew his weakness, sweets! As he walked over to the coffee machine, he could hear the night people talking. Roselle and Joan were sitting at their "retiree table." Lenny heard Roselle say something about her daughter. Holy shit! She said her daughter thinks someone is killing the "retiree table" people! Did he hear her right? Sometimes he was so paranoid! He nonchalantly moved closer to their table to try and hear better. They stopped talking to each other and started talking to him. Damn it! He thought. I'm sure that's what I heard. Shit! I don't want to have to kill her daughter too! Roselle asked him "do you like the brownies, because I just brought them in to work?" He told her "yes, they're very chocolatey. They're perfect with a cup of coffee. Thank you for bringing them in here." Roselle answered him "no problem, I'm planning on baking a lot after I retire." Lenny smiled at the two of them and went back to his office. In his head he was thinking... You won't be baking shit! His killer personality was so crass. Maybe he was becoming schizophrenic. All he knew was....He was ready to be done with all of it. Come on Wednesday!

# CHAPTER 42

Lenny went past Roselle's house last night. The first time he went by he watched the neighbor's windows. He wasn't surprised when he saw a white haired old woman looking out the window. That's just how they are: they listen for cars going by. She was probably telling her husband "come look, there's a car out here on our street." He would probably answer "who cares. It's a public street" because that's how men are. We could care less about the traffic out on the street. Lenny hoped him and Cindy lived to be that old together. That old woman looking out her window kept Lenny from stopping and trying to sneak in or even to knock on the door and look in the windows. While driving in her neighborhood he noticed there was a chicken restaurant a block away and a college about five hundred feet across the street. He shouldn't have any problems parking his car and walking to Roselle's house. He might just go down her street and park though because it would be dark. The college and the chicken restaurant were fairly well lit. He was going to need a cover of darkness. He needed to look in his closet and see if he had any black shirts. He knew he had some black jeans.

Jeans were so much better for killing; he wouldn't feel right killing Roselle in his dress pants. He had to chuckle to himself when he replayed what he was just thinking in his head. Who was he? My goodness worrying about what was better to wear while killing someone! Those kids weren't around either last night. They must have had some home work. They probably thought he was stalking them. Nah kids are stupid they probably got to riding their bikes and forgot all about him. That's what he was hoping anyway.

Roselle and Joan were sitting at the "retiree table" talking about the train trip Roselle wanted to go on. She wanted to wait till Joan and her husband, Don, retired and they could all go together. Joan liked the idea of going to Las Vegas and knew she could talk her husband into that trip. She reminded Roselle that "we have two more years till we can retire. They had it all planned out and were sticking to their plan." Roselle told her "that's fine; it will give me plenty of time to research everything we'll want to see. If there's something Don wants to see, let me know so I can put it on our itinerary. I know I want to see a couple shows and maybe go see the Grand Canyon while we're so close." Joan said "yes! The Grand Canyon is a definite choice. Don will want to gamble too." Roselle told her "me too! It wouldn't be Las Vegas if we didn't gamble!"

Then they started to talk about Bobbie's ridiculous idea of their friends being murdered. Roselle said "I know, she watches a lot of crime shows on television." Joan said "haha yeah, all the autopsies proved otherwise. Did you tell her that?" Roselle said "yes I did, but she still doesn't believe me. She reads a lot of books too. She's never going to believe me." Joan said "did you know Janice's son never came and got her stuff out of her locker?" Roselle told her "no I never realized that. I guess we could clean it out for him and take it over to her house. We could do it on last break. Janice told me the combination to her locker after the fiasco with Mary." Joan told her "ok, can you take it over there tomorrow? I don't think she has a lot here, probably a sweater and a couple books. That's probably why he hasn't come in to clean it out. He might not even know she has a locker." Roselle told Joan "yes, I can run it over there tomorrow morning."

Last Break was finally here. The two of them went to Janice's locker and cleaned it out Joan was right, there really wasn't a lot in it. The only personal thing was her sweater; the rest was just books that they knew Janice would want them to read. They decided to call her son and ask if he wanted the sweater. He answered the phone and Joan told him about cleaning out his mom's locker and that the only thing she really had in it was a sweater. He asked her if they could just donate it to charity because he had so much stuff to go through at home. She asked him if he was going to be able to handle it and he told her his sister was going to come over and help him. She thought that was a good idea. She wasn't sure she would want a male high school senior going through her things if something happened to her. He was her son, but there are things boys don't understand that women have in their closets, her daughter would understand. She told him they were all praying for him and if he needed anything he could call her or Roselle. They put her sweater in the lost and found box for someone who forgot theirs, so they could go and borrow it.

Bobbie and Tj were sitting on their swing talking that evening. It was such a nice night; the air was cool but not cold. The stars were out too. Bobbie told him her idea of the women being killed and not dying of natural causes or whatever the autopsies said, and that her mom thought she watched too many crime shows on television. Tj told her "they couldn't have been killed. They all died different ways. If someone was killing them, they would have all died the same way." He added "that's how serial killers worked." he didn't watch a lot of her shows with her but he could hear them while she watched them. Bobbie said "I just think it's too coincidental, something's up. I don't know that I could ever prove anything but I just don't feel right about it. Plus her boss creeps me out! I met him at the viewing for Marge. Something's not right about that guy!" Tj started laughing "ha! Are you serious? Now you think it's her boss! Your moms right, you really are watching too many crime shows!" Bobbie didn't bring it up again. She couldn't get anyone to believe her. She thought this is bullshit, why can't they see it!

# CHAPTER 43

Finally it's Wednesday! Lenny was getting excited way too early! He had all day to get through first. He really needed to think about how he was going to get in Roselle's house. He knew he had to get in without that old lady across the street watching him. The bitch had to go to bed sometime!

Cindy got up and made him breakfast. Ham and eggs, the breakfast of champions. Champion killers he thought in his head. She was telling him today was her first day to volunteer in Kathy's classroom, she was so excited. He was happy for her; sometimes the kids in the hospital depressed her. They didn't always live and it broke her heart. He hated seeing her so sad. That sucked because he knew he was going to be the cause of her being sad soon. She really liked Roselle and respected her volunteerism spirit. She was a giving person, hell they both were giving people! He hated doing this to Cindy, but it had to be done. He knew he wasn't taking the money out of his own accounts. Piss on that noise he thought. He got dressed after breakfast and went into work. Cindy got dressed and went to the school. She was super excited to get to work with her friend and with a bunch of healthy kids.

Roselle got up this morning and made herself a cup of tea and a piece of toast. She had a doctor appointment this morning. Good thing she didn't have to go to Janice's. She had forgotten about her appointment last night when she was talking to Joan. She went out on her enclosed patio and drank her tea. Then she had to get in the shower and get ready for her doctor appointment. She was hoping that she had lost some weight. She was riding her bike every night, not for very long but definitely every night! She could feel a difference in how much stronger her legs were. She was dressed and on her way to the doctor.

Bobbie had to work this morning. She kind of liked that too. It meant she could spend the evening with Tj and the kids. Mom would probably come over for supper too since it was her day off.

Everyone was busy at work or school today. The husbands were all at work. The sisters were all at work. The kids were all in school. It was your regular run of the mill humdrum day.

Lenny had to figure out what time he was going to go to Roselle's house. He also needed to get some wine for him and Cindy tonight. He was hoping she was having a great day so she would want to celebrate tonight.

Cindy was having an outstanding day! She absolutely loved working with Kathy's classroom. The kids were great and they all warmed up to her quickly. She wished she would have done this years ago. She was even thinking, maybe she should go back to school and get a degree doing something with kids. She wasn't sure teaching is what she wanted, but there had to be something she could do. She was going to stop and get some wine on her way home and a nice juicy steak for her and Lenny. She wanted to celebrate how wonderful her day had been!

Roselle was at the doctor. This was the first time she ever wanted to get on the scales. She had been eating better because Bobbie made her suppers every night. She also had been riding that stationary bike every day too. She got on the scale... Yay she lost ten pounds! Wow imagine what she'll lose when she rides it longer after she retires. She wanted it to be more but she always wanted it to be more. She decided to be happy about the ten pounds. The doctor wanted her to get a flu shot today too. She was in such a good mood she told them "why not." She got her flu shot and blood work for her diabetes. Then she was on her way home.

Being a Wednesday at Bobbie's work, that meant it was senior citizens day. She loved having all the seniors in the store. Some of her workmates didn't like it. They said the old people walk too slow, talk too slow, do everything too slow. Bobbie reminded them that we're all going to get old someday if we're lucky. They had to agree with that. The senior citizens liked to talk but Bobbie didn't mind that. She loved to talk. She had some seniors that would come to the shoe department every Wednesday, just to visit. She called them her regulars with pride.

Roselle would come in on Wednesdays too. She was a senior citizen; at least the cashiers would always give her the discount. They just knew she was Bobbie's mom and that was enough for them. They probably gave all the employees parents the discount. Bobbie was glad mom came in because she would buy her lunch at the cafe in the store. She also helped her pick up the shoe department. People would try shoes on and not put them back on the shelves. Bobbie didn't mind it on Wednesdays because usually it was a senior citizen and they didn't bend as well anymore to pick them up. That didn't stop her from having her mom help her though. She didn't make her help; she just liked spending time with Bobbie. They could talk while they picked shoes up. Roselle always had a little shopping to do too. She loved to shop, whether it was shoes or blankets, didn't matter. She would tell you "it's a girl thing." All of Roselle's daughters and granddaughters liked to shop. In their family, it really was a girl thing! The guys in the family were into sports and science fiction. Football, baseball and aliens were their main topics of conversation. Computers were starting to become popular. Tj had to buy one, but it was so bulky and took up too much space in their dining room. Bobbie hated it! The kids and Tj loved it; they would play games on it. Two chairs and two joysticks meant an enjoyable rainy afternoon to them.

# CHAPTER 44

Lenny was looking at his watch all day. Was this day ever going to get to the evening? Holy crap it's only four o'clock! He decided to leave anyway. He was the boss around here. The store was on his way home and he wanted to get a bottle of wine for tonight. He went in and got three nice steaks and a bottle of wine. He also went to a fast food restaurant and bought a big salad for the two of them to share. One steak was for Roselle's dog. He almost forgot to buy it a steak. He was glad he didn't. That was something he was really going to need tonight.

Cindy was already home when he pulled into the garage. He forgot school gets out at two thirty. She said "hey I stopped and bought us a bottle of wine and a steak on my way home. We need to celebrate tonight. I absolutely loved being around all those second graders." Lenny said "haha great minds think alike, I did the same thing! I stopped and bought a salad for us to share too." He held his purchases up so she could see them. They both thought it was pretty funny and had their first glass of wine together to toast her day. Why not? They had two bottles of wine. It was going to get drunk out tonight. Yes! Thought Lenny. Once she had a couple glasses she'll never notice that she's the only one drinking.

Roselle did go to Bobbies for supper. She pulled up out front and could see grunt in the storm door wagging his butt. She had his bones in her pocket and gave them to him. They were having spaghetti and garlic bread for supper. Bobbie had the sauce cooking all day in the crock pot. She baked a big spaghetti squash instead of noodles, to make it healthier. It smelled like Italy when you walked in the door. "Yum that smells delicious" said Roselle. Bobbie told her "I know, I made it in the crockpot because Liddy has a softball game tonight at six, and I had to work today. Do you want to come with us to watch the game?" Roselle said "I don't know, I've been busy all day. The doctor gave me a flu shot today and my arm is killing me. I think I'll just go home after we eat." She was looking at the game schedule magnetized to the fridge. "Tell Liddy I'll go to her game next Monday. Ok?" Bobbie asked "are you sure mom? I'll tell her about Monday's game though, she'll be glad to have you there." Roselle told Bobbie "yes I'm sure about tonight, but I will be there Monday!" They ate dinner together, just Roselle and Bobbie and Tj. Then she left and went home and they got ready to go to Liddys game. She was the catcher and they were very proud of her!

When Roselle got home, she had a couple hours of daylight left. She rode her bike, then grabbed her book and went on her patio. She read for a couple hours and finally finished the book she was reading. Then she thought about going inside to watch wrestling. She used to take her daughters to the wrestling matches when they were young. They all loved it too and had autographs from a lot of the wrestlers. That's probably the reason behind Bobbie thinking she was a bad ass, she thought with a smile. It was dark outside now. She went in and settled in for the night with wrestling on the television.

Lenny was getting excited, the drunker Cindy got. He knew she would pass out easy tonight. He had his dark clothes ready to go, in his closet. It was getting close to eleven o'clock. He crushed the sleeping pill between two spoons and put it in her wine glass. She drank a whole bottle by herself, this should be easy. He told her he had to be up early and was going to bed. She said she didn't have to go to the school tomorrow, it was every other day. "Good thing too, I'm probably going to have a hangover tomorrow from all this wine. Do you mind if I watch the television in our room?" Lenny told her "of course not, come on up" he knew she would be passing out soon anyway. She was out cold before she could even decide what she wanted to watch. Perfect! Thought Lenny. He changed his clothes, grabbed his steak out of the refrigerator, and drove to Roselle's house. Thank God Cindy was so excited about her day. She didn't even notice the extra steak he bought. The syringe was already in his pocket. He put it there yesterday. Driving over there he could hardly contain his excitement. Soon he would be finished with all this nonsense. The money would be back in the executive pension fund and he wouldn't have to worry about any of his friends retiring.

The old people across the street must be in bed. There weren't any lights on at their house. Lenny decided to park on Roselle's street a couple houses down. It looked like everyone was asleep. There was a television light coming from Roselle's house. He went in the gate and looked in the window. She was lying on the sofa. He then went around to the back patio, not the enclosed one on the side of the house. This patio had a fence around it but no roof. There were patio doors back here. He slid it to see if it opened. It did! I swear I really need to have a safety talk with these women! He had his steak in his hand, carrying it by the bone, for the dog but no dog was coming. It must not be a very good watchdog, maybe it's asleep. He walked through the room the patio doors were in and was in her hallway. Still no dog, he set the steak on her dining room table. He looked into her living room. It was actually all one big room. She had a stationary bike in there. He could hear her snoring. Yes! She was asleep. She looked asleep when he looked in the window, but she could have just been resting her eyes. Could he get any luckier? This was going to be as easy as all the others had been he thought. Crap! He ran into the chair at the table, she started stirring. Shit, shit, shit! He didn't want her to wake up! Damn it she was getting up! He felt like a deer caught in the headlights. He was in her living room then. He had no idea where he could hide. She saw him. At first it startled her then she realized it was Lenny from work. She said "Lenny, what the hell are you doing here? In my house!" Lenny didn't know what to say. He finally said "look Rosie, I didn't want to have to do this like this. I embezzled money and need your pension to pay it back". Roselle was pissed "you son of a bitch! You're not getting a penny of my money! I worked hard for that pension!" He lunged for her and she tried to kick him in the balls, missed but got away from him. She saw the syringe. She said "you mother fucker you did kill them didn't you! Bobbie was right! Roselle knew there was no pleading; the look in his eyes told her everything Bobbie said was true! He wouldn't stop till she was dead. Lenny was thinking damn it; all I have to do is get this syringe in her. She pushed her stationary bike into him. He put the syringe back in his pocket for safe keeping. He didn't want her knocking it out of his hand. He grabbed her arm but couldn't squeeze too much. He didn't want to leave any marks. She fell and he was on the floor too. She got him in a scissor hold with her new found strong legs. Son of a bitch she was stronger than he gave her credit for! Where the hell did she get this strength from he thought? He looked at the television and saw the wrestling match, aha it clicked! Damn, she was squeezing him so tight he could hardly breathe. She had her legs locked around him and her feet crossed tight! Watching wrestling finally paid off! She was hoping she could break him in half, she was so pissed! He tried to get her legs out from around him. She was punching him too; she was one strong old lady! He didn't know where this strength was coming from. There was no budging her. He pulled the syringe back out of his pocket, even though he could barely breathe. She saw it too late and couldn't get away from him or knock it out of his hands. She figured better to at least break some ribs because she knew she wouldn't make it to her phone to call the police. She squeezed as tight as she could as she still tried to knock it out of his hand. She was practically on her side squeezing him. He put it in her thigh and pushed the plunger! Whew he thought, a couple minutes and this would be all over. Her legs loosened from being so tight around him. He was thinking, she broke my fucking ribs. He got up and straightened her house back up. Made it look like no one was ever there. He picked her up from the floor and guided her to her couch. She was the only one he apologized to, "I'm sorry Rosie, and I really didn't want to kill you like this." He was sore though and almost didn't apologize but he did understand how angry she was, He would've been! She was the only one he killed who knew they were being killed. He knew she had spunk! She answered him "fuck you! Karma knows where you live you bastard and she'll be coming for you!" He smiled at that response. She was still alive but not for long, she was already at the chest pain stage. He grabbed his steak and got out of there. He went out of the house the same way he went in. After he left, she felt like he was still fighting her. Her chest was so tight. She called Bobbies house with her phone that was on the floor by the sofa. Roselle wanted to tell her she was right and it was her boss doing the killing! Tj answered and she said real faint "I can't breathe". Tj couldn't understand her, he said "Rose, is that you?" She tried to say it again. He tossed the phone to Bobbie. "I think it's your mom, I can't hear her". When Bobbie put the phone to her ear she could hear her mom moaning faintly. Bobbie thought she must have fallen. Tj was already getting dressed and she grabbed her clothes and got most of herself dressed real quickly. They jumped in the car and headed over to moms house. They thought they would get there and she would be on the floor unable to get up. Bobbie was hoping she didn't break a hip or something. She heard that was really painful. They would take her to the hospital and get her fixed up.

# CHAPTER 45

It took Tj and Bobbie about eight minutes to get to Roselle's. Bobbie finished getting dressed in the car. Normally it took ten minutes but they ran most of the stop signs in their neighborhood. When they got there it wasn't what they expected to see. They thought she had fallen and broke her hip or leg, something they could handle. The way she moaned on the phone was like when she fell and broke her ankle a couple years ago.

Mom was on the couch, the television was on with a wrestling tape in the VCR. Bobbie ran to her. She had foam coming out of her mouth and nose. Bobbie checked for a pulse, nothing. She called 911 for an ambulance. Part of her knew she was gone there was no life in her eyes. They were open but lifeless. There was no pulse in her wrist or neck. Bobbie had tears running down her face as she told her mom to hang on, the ambulance was coming. She was smoothing her mom's hands as she told her "if there's any part of you left in there, hang on! The ambulance will be here soon. Don't die mom! They could use those paddle things and bring her back to life. Tj knew she was gone and went down the street to get Valerie and Jim. Bobbie was crying, not a soft cry more like sobbing. When Val and Jim got there, Valerie was crying. Tj called Emily too but she had to come twenty miles. The ambulance finally arrived. Bobbie thought it took forever. Tj told her it had been less than five minutes and probably only three minutes. It always seems longer when you need them now. Bobbie told them her mom had called her house and was moaning, like she fell or something. If she would have known this was what was going on, she would've called 911 from her house. They looked at Roselle and knew she'd been gone for at least twenty minutes. They checked for a pulse on her wrists, her neck and her feet, nothing. They did that to appease the family, but she was gone and they knew it as soon as they walked in the door. They broke the news to Bobbie and Valerie that nothing would have saved her. Bobbie asked about the foam and they said she must've had fluid in her heart or lungs. Bobbie knew she had congestive heart disease. They were both crying. Bobbie told them she only had one more week to work and she would've retired. It wasn't fair! The ambulance guys didn't think it was fair either. They also wondered how in the heck she called her daughter; she was gone for at least twenty minutes when they got there. They figured the kids must've had their timing off. It was her angel that called her daughter. There was no other way to explain it. Bobbie asked them if it was possibly murder. The ambulance attendants couldn't or wouldn't say, they said it was definitely a heart attack. They called the coroner. He came and pronounced her dead and had the body transported to the morgue. By then Emily and Cam got there. Bobbie and Tj told them what happened. Emily asked "why didn't mom call Val's house?" Bobbie told her "I don't know, we were wondering the same thing" Val didn't understand it either. She was only a block away. Tj said "why didn't she call 911?" Nothing made any sense. She used her last breath to call Bobbie. A breath she didn't really have. By then all of mom's neighbors were outside wondering why they had all these red and blue lights reflecting on their houses. When they saw it was an ambulance and they found out mom had passed away, they all gave their condolences and went back home to bed. Nobody saw the stranger in their neighborhood. Nobody knew to look for a stranger. Nobody heard him park his car and get out and close his door. Nobody saw him walk to Roselle's house and go in the patio doors. They were all in bed sleeping. Bobbie knew there had to be a reason her mom called her ten minutes away and not Val who was only a block away. Right now she was in shock. She couldn't even think. All she wanted to do was curl up and cry some more. They all went home to their own houses after the coroner left, and they'd talked for at least an hour outside of mom's house. Bobbie told her sisters, "Mom had a doctor appointment today and was fine. She came to our house for supper, nothing was wrong with her, she was a little tired but that's it, and that could've been from the flu shot." Bobbie knew one thing, she was calling the coroner in the morning and telling them she wanted a full autopsy! She wanted to know why her mom died. She wanted a full toxicology report. Everything that was in her system! She felt like her whole world had just crashed! The sadness overwhelmed her. She couldn't even kill a fly because she thought, what if it's mom's spirit? That was so silly, but that's how she felt. It was like her own soul had been ripped from her body. She couldn't do any dishes by hand because the soap suds reminded her of her mom, and would start her crying again. The thought of the foam gave her nightmares. It was the worst time of her life. Her eyes were always red. She would be fine one minute and the next, tears would be flowing. Sometimes all it took was someone saying how sorry they were and she would be crying. She hated the thought of going back to work.

Emily and Bobbie called the family and friends the next morning. They called them around six A.M. None of them slept that night. Bobbie called Joan and told her the sad news. Joan didn't say anything then about it possibly being murder. She knew the girls were hurting and that they would have time to talk in the coming days. She was really starting to agree with Bobbie though! Emily worked for herself but Bobbie had to call her work and tell them that she wouldn't be in to work and why. Valerie had to call her work too so did all their husbands. Bobbie wasn't sure she would ever sleep and she couldn't eat. Tj was worried about her and called their doctor for something to calm her down. Bobbie called the coroner and told him she wanted a full autopsy. She wanted to know why her mom died! That afternoon Emily and Bobbie and Valerie went to the local funeral home and made arrangements for their mom. The funeral home had a room full of caskets to choose from. They all ended up at the same one. It was pink with a Rose on top. They knew mom would love this one. It felt like she drew them to it. They asked about music because their mom loved country music. The funeral home said if they had a couple tapes they could play them during the viewing. Mom would like that, they thought. Grandma and aunt Dolly had to come in from Texas. Their uncles were only coming from Ohio. Mom's friends were all local. The sisters decided to have the viewing Friday and the burial on Saturday.

Lenny could hardly walk, his ribs hurt so bad. He couldn't believe how strong Roselle was. She truly surprised him as much as he surprised her. She must use that bike she had in her living room! He wasn't sure if he could fool people about his sincerity on her death. She was a bitch to kill. She was a fighter! She had wrestling on the television and must've been pretty serious about it. He couldn't believe she cussed either. He always thought she was a sweet little old lady. I guess that changes when someone's trying to kill you he thought. The way his ribs felt, he hoped he could work tomorrow. Damn! She must've freaking broke some, at least one! He was in serious pain. He should've known he couldn't get lucky again! He kept thinking of the look on her face when he told her about embezzling the pension money. She was pissed! He never in the thirty three years he'd known her saw her that angry. He smiled when it dawned on him that he wouldn't see her angry again. She was done being angry. She did say one thing that threw him for a loop. She said Bobbie was right. At that moment he remembered hearing her and Joan talk the other day. He did hear her right. Shit! He hoped he wasn't going to have to kill her daughter. They would most certainly do an autopsy and he knew it wouldn't say anything about poison. He was so thankful that he hadn't used the rat poison. He'd been through the autopsy thing before. He wasn't going to worry about that at all. Now he had to sneak back into his house and change back into pajamas without waking Cindy. It shouldn't be a problem but with the luck he had tonight, he wasn't counting on it.

# CHAPTER 46

The girls had to find something for their mom to wear for the funeral. Emily found a pretty blue dress in mom's closet, but Bobbie told her "that wouldn't work." Mom had recently told her if she died she wanted to be buried in a fringe dress. Emily said "what do you mean if she died?" Bobbie told her "I told mom, I think someone was killing the women she worked with. There were too many deaths recently, all out of her office!" Valerie said "I gotta agree with that. I don't know about murders but there were definitely a lot of them dying." Emily asked Bobbie "did you call the coroner?" "You bet I did! We will get a full report from him!" Said Bobbie. They decided to go to the mall in town. They had been in what seemed like a thousand million specialty dress stores and no luck. Then they went to the department store in the mall, not thinking they would have any luck. Valerie and Emily were ready to give up on the idea of a fringe dress when Bobbie found one. That was the first time she'd smiled in it seemed like days. Imagine that, smiling because you found the perfect dress to bury your mom in, the tears started to fall. They all had a little cry together then bought the dress. Bobbie knew if mom was looking down on them that she would be smiling. They all bought themselves a new outfit too. Emily got a red pant suit because that was her favorite color. Valerie bought a green dress and Bobbie bought a purple pantsuit. They wanted to be in colors mom knew they loved. They had to buy a burial spot too. There was a cemetery in Osceola with a church across the street with a big white cross on it that mom always liked. She never really said why she liked it but they called it and were able to get a plot for mom. Bobbie told them she wanted it by a tree so mom could have shade. Her sisters thought she was crazy, but she felt pretty strong about it. The cemetery said they had a plot by a tree, not to worry about it. They also said that they get that request more than you would think. Then they went to the florist and ordered a mother flower arrangement for at the funeral home. They also bought a grandma arrangement for all of the grand kids.

When they arrived early for the viewing, they couldn't believe all the flowers and plants people sent. There was a huge arrangement from moms work too. There were tons of flowers. People who knew mom knew she loved flowers, maybe that's why there were so many. The sisters couldn't believe how many people were at the viewing. Moms work closed their office and made calls go through a satellite office. Everyone was there! They never saw so many people at a funeral. They knew mom was friends with everyone. There were people from work; people from the soup kitchen, people mom grew up with. There were even old neighbors from other places they lived growing up. She made an impression on so many people. You never realize how many people you touch when you're alive. That brought tears to Bobbie's eyes. Thank God Emily was so strong. She stationed herself at mom's coffin and talked to people as they viewed mom and said a prayer. Bobbie couldn't have talked to so many people without crying. She was a basket case. She talked to people in the room but on her terms. She needed to be able to cry in between people. Bobbie probably went through a whole box of tissues by herself. She was the closest to mom. All of her friends had stories about their mom that they shared with the girls. Their own friends from work were there too. Jackie and her husband came and gave their condolences. Collette and her boyfriend came too. It was nice having her friends there. They both wanted to ask Bobbie if she thought her mom was killed like she had told them about some of the women her mom worked with. They didn't bring it up though. They knew there would be a time and a place where the three of them could talk. Aunt Dolly and grandma made it in plenty of time. They brought aunt Dolly's son too. He looked more like Josh's brother than Michael did. He acted like josh too. They were only a year apart. The three boys hung together the whole time. Their uncles made it too. Their uncle Ralph and his wife, Judy from their dad's side was there too. They knew him better than they did their dad. The viewing was exhausting for Bobbie. She liked seeing everyone but seeing her mom in the coffin was hard. She didn't want to leave the room. This would be the last time she would ever get to see her. She still couldn't believe her mom was gone. Now more than ever she thought it was murder!

People filtered in and out the whole four hours. There was a break in between but Bobbie stayed with her mom. Actually all three of the sisters stayed. Their husbands went with their kids and got them something to eat. All their lives, she was all they really ever had. Mom's family all lived out of state except

Uncle David and he died quite a few years ago. He didn't live in the same town either. They didn't have a close relationship with any of them. Aunt Dolly was the closest, she stayed in contact with them but she lived in Texas and you can't just go there to talk about boys or stuff that girls needed to talk about. It was nice to see her but this wasn't a good time to catch up with her.

Moms boss Lenny and his wife came too. Her name was Cindy; Bobbie met her at a volunteer luncheon. She seemed nice and was very upset. Her husband made Bobbie very uncomfortable. He just creeped her out, the hair on her arms even stood up. Something wasn't right about that guy! He looked like he was in pain too. When Bill, the Vice President of moms work came in and gave Lenny a hug, he looked like he was going to die right there. Bobbie watched him as he talked to Bill. She went closer to listen in on their conversation. He was telling him that he fell and thought he might have some broken ribs. Bill asked him why he hadn't gone to the hospital. Lenny said he thought it was going to get better on its own and didn't like doctors. Bill told him he needed to get it looked at. They could give him painkillers at least. Bobbie wondered why anyone would not go to the hospital if they thought they had broken ribs. What an idiot, she thought, especially if it's from a fall. Then the three of them went to talk to the women from work and Bobbie went to Tj. She needed a hug. There were groups of women mom worked with everywhere. Some were crying, some were laughing as they told stories about mom. She was a funny lady and loved a good laugh. If her spirit was here she would've been happy about all the people who came to celebrate her life.

The viewing was over before Bobbie was ready to leave her mom. She looked so pretty in her black fringe dress. Nobody knew the sisters decided to bury her in her slippers. Mom hated shoes and would be happy when she got to heaven and had her comfy slippers on. The grandkids had all put things in her coffin. They put pictures and angel figurines and small things their grandma would like when she got to heaven. Bobbie thought she would take one of the pills Tj got her tonight and sleep. She couldn't help hoping mom would visit her in her dreams.

# CHAPTER 47

Bobbie never did take the pill Tj got for her. After the viewing the whole family went to a buffet restaurant. Grandma and her aunt and uncles were all hungry. Bobbie liked that it was just family. They had been around so many people all evening. She just needed a quiet peaceful supper. She really didn't eat much; she still had a hard time enjoying food when mom couldn't. The guilt was too much. After someone close dies you feel guilt if you're having a good time. You can't laugh or joke without that guilty feeling. At least Bobbie couldn't. Her eyes were red from all the crying she'd been doing. They all ate supper; the husbands all enjoyed seeing the family. It broke some of the sadness their wives were having. Uncle Charlie told the girls he wanted to sing at the funeral. They were all ok with it. Emily wanted to speak at the funeral too. Bobbie didn't know how she did it. There was no way Bobbie could go in front of all those people and talk about mom without crying and not being able to finish speaking. Valerie couldn't speak in front of them either. They were both glad Emily was so strong because they all felt one of them should talk at the funeral. It was getting late and they had the funeral service at eleven the next morning. Soon they finished eating and they all went home. Mom's family was staying in a hotel. None of the girl's homes were big enough to have them all stay there.

The funeral service was today. Bobbie wearily got dressed. She still hadn't slept very much. It was misting outside, and she thought well that's great, my hair is going to frizz up for the funeral. Then felt guilty she was even worrying about her hair. Mom couldn't worry about her hair. The tears were already starting. Tj gave her a big hug and told her don't worry about it. She was beautiful no matter what her hair looked like. He told her he liked it when it was frizzy anyway. She loved him so much, she was glad she had him beside her for all of this. She didn't even bother with any makeup. It would be useless; she knew she would cry it off. She made sure the kids all looked good and they were on their way. Tj grabbed a couple umbrellas too, just in case they needed them at the burial.

When they arrived at the funeral home, they couldn't believe all the cars that were lined up already. There had to be fifty cars in line already. Wow! They were there early too. Bobbie was hoping to get some alone time with mom. That wasn't going to happen. They had Valerie's pastor giving the sermon. Mom was divorced and the Catholic Church shunned people who were divorced. Mom had decided piss on them she wasn't staying married for her church. She never went back to the Catholic Church after the divorce other than a few times of midnight mass at Christmas. The sisters talked to the pastor about mom a couple days ago. He had lots of stories he could use for his sermon. Uncle Charlie was planning on singing during the procession. Emily would speak after the pastor talked.

Everyone was seated. The funeral home had to bring more chairs into the room. Mom knew so many people! The place was packed and even had some people standing in the back. Bobbie never realized how popular her mom was until now. The pastor spoke, and said a prayer. He then passed the floor to Emily. She read from a speech she had written. Bobbie was so proud of her. She couldn't have done that. She was crying throughout Emily's speech. Tj held her hand the whole time. She leaned into him the whole service. She really just wanted to curl up on his lap and have a good cry. She saw that Lenny guy there too. He never shed a tear, his wife was crying though. For a second Bobbie thought, what a creep! After Emily was finished they started the procession and Uncle Charlie sang the song about a cross. He sang better than Bobbie thought he would. The family was first. Bobbie didn't want to leave her, but Tj whispered that there were a lot of other people who needed to say good bye too. So she moved on slowly. After everyone was through. All the son in laws and Bobbies boys and Uncle Charlie were the pall bearers. Uncle Tom had a problem with funerals and waited outside. He had seen too many friends die over his lifetime.

Then it was a long drive to the cemetery. There were at least seventy five cars in the line going there. People on the streets were going to be mad because the procession was so long. They had the right of way. It was going to be a long wait at the stop lights for them. They would think it was someone really important. It was someone important! It's my mom and she's very important! That's how Bobbie felt about it.

They arrived at the cemetery; cars were lined up on the street because it was such a small cemetery. They had chairs set up for grandma and the sisters underneath a canopy. It was raining; Bobbie figured it was the angels crying for mom. All the flowers were there too. The funeral home would deliver the house plants to Bobbie's house later that day. The pastor said a short sermon and said a prayer. Then each of the sisters threw a rose on the casket. They lowered the casket into the hole that was dug already. The people were leaving, it was over. That was the end of their mom. Bobbie didn't want to leave till they actually buried her. Tj told her they don't cover the casket with anyone there. They wait till everyone is gone. He was thinking, it's too final when they cover it and some people can't take it. She certainly wouldn't be able to see that and he knew it. He ushered her to their car.

Everyone was meeting at Tj and Bobbie's house for a meal together. People brought so much food to her house. Even moms creepy boss brought two big meat trays for sandwiches. Bobbie thought maybe he's not so bad after all. He brought them himself instead of having them delivered. Lenny was thinking, he wanted to see the layout of Bobbie's house, just in case, He heard anymore about murders. This is where the dog lived that he saw at Roselle's the day he drove by in the morning. He left before the game started. All their cousins and family and some of mom's friends came over. Tj asked Bobbie if she thought they could turn the college football game on the television. At first she didn't want to, she thought it was disrespectful. Then she thought bullshit, mom would be pissed if they didn't have the game on, Tj agreed and turned the television on to the game. He ate watching the game. Bobbie sat at the table with her sisters and other family. All the guys were with Tj though. Mom was probably in there too, she thought with a small smile.

After the game grandma wanted pictures since all the cousins and everyone else was there. Bobbie reluctantly got in the pictures with her red eyes. She wondered if there was ever going to be a day when she didn't tear up and have such red eyes. Grandma was right to take pictures though because everyone was there. The kids were all dressed up and looked nice. Perfect time for pictures, except mom wasn't in them. While they were on the front porch taking pictures for grandma, the funeral home delivered the potted plants. Holy crap thought Bobbie, what are we going to do with all these plants? Her and her sisters each kept a couple and gave the others to friends and family members that wanted one. There were so many. Bobbie could feel mom's spirit and thought see how much people loved you mom. She just knew her mom was smiling.

# CHAPTER 48

Lenny took two meat trays to Roselle's after funeral dinner. Cindy thought that was very thoughtful of him since Roselle was the highest seniority person in his building. He especially wanted to take them himself when he found out that they were all meeting at Bobbies house. He didn't trust her! She looked like a younger version of Roselle and probably acted like her too. He decided he could kill her too if he had to. She did have a dog and kids and a husband in the house though. He figured he would have to do it away from home, if he had to do it all. The coroner's report would most likely say heart attack. For some reason he didn't think Bobbie was going to believe that. If she started digging around, he was going to have to be ready. Now he wished he would've made three syringes instead of the two he did make. She looked super healthy though and no one would believe it if she died of a heart attack. He would have to think of something else.

He and Cindy pulled up to their house and Bill was waiting for them. Crap Lenny forgot the two of them had made plans to watch the game together today. Bill told him "let's order pizza for the game."Can you believe Roselle had a heart attack too? They're falling like flies around here" Lenny gave him a look that said, I know. Cindy let them order pizza; she went to her craft room. She wasn't in the mood for football, or to listen to them talk about it either.

Bobbie and her sisters met at their moms the next day. They had to get a game plan for getting it ready to sell. Valerie thought her mom's bike was in the wrong place. She would know too because she rode it every time she came over. Bobbie looked and Val was right. It had been in the same spot so long it left a mark on the floor. It definitely wasn't in its right place. They asked each other, do you think mom would've moved it? Bobbie hopped on it and said "no, mom wouldn't have moved it here, you can't even see the television and you know she had to watch her wrestling!" They left it where it was. Bobbie asked Val to go get her camera from her house. When she got back with her camera they took a lot of pictures. Pictures of where the bike should have been, and where it was now. After seeing the bike was definitely moved, Bobbie went in all the rooms to see if anything else had been displaced. When she went in the room with the sliding doors, she knew someone had been in mom's house. She yelled "Val, bring your camera back here. The sliding door wasn't closed all the way! Someone was here and I know it! I knew somebody killed mom's friends and mom too!" Val and Emily said "don't jump to conclusions, mom could've done it." Emily said "yeah, we know she never locked any of her dang doors." Val agreed with Emily. They also thought the ambulance people probably moved her bike too. Bobbie didn't believe any of it though. She knew somebody was killing people, but she didn't know who. Bobbie asked Val to take a picture of the sliding door anyway. She was going to get to the bottom of this if it took her whole life. What she didn't know was that it just might take her life! She wanted to talk to her friends Collette and Jackie. She had been telling them about her mom's friends. They knew the whole story. After they all left their mom's house, without disturbing anything, she went home. She didn't think Val and Emily believed her about a killer running loose. She knew her friends did though!

Once she got home, she remembered she had to call the restaurant and cancel mom's party. It brought tears to her eyes telling them she was canceling because she passed away. Lori already knew not to make the cake because she was at the funeral. Emily could talk to her friend Maria about the piñata. That was the end of that, I guess. She was glad she got those calls over with. Now she could concentrate on finding a killer. She's was going back to moms tomorrow by herself.

She was hoping Jackie and Collette would meet her there. She didn't want her sisters going because they didn't think anything was wrong. How could they not see it thought Bobbie it's so freaking obvious! Mom hadn't believed her either. She decided to call Joan and see what she thought. She was totally surprised that Joan agreed with her. Joan thought it's too coincidental, all those women from their office. Bobbie asked her to keep her ears open. She let her know that there was something about their boss Lenny that creeped her out. Bobbie said when he came to the visitation, the hair on her arms stood up. Joan didn't know what to think of that, but she said he's injured and he said he fell but he doesn't have any bruises. None that they can see, he does usually wear his suit coat though. Joan and the women she hung around with now think he has broken ribs. He's still taking the stairs though instead of the elevator because he thinks no one notices his injury. He always looks like he's in deep thought all the time too. Joan said like if no one was around him, he would be talking to himself. Bobbie asked her to really keep an eye on him now. That's suspicious behavior, like he's guilty of something!

The coroner's office called Bobbie and told her the autopsy paperwork was finished and she could pick it up anytime. She went right over there to get it. Damn! It said myocardial infarction. In other words, a heart attack. She couldn't believe it! She asked about the toxicology report and was told nothing unusual was found in her system. They said she had high sodium counts but that wasn't unusual for someone who had a heart attack. Too much sodium isn't good for you. Well crap, Bobbie wasn't sure what to do now. She knows someone killed her mom and the more she hears, the more she thinks it's Lenny, her moms boss! He isn't getting away with this!

# CHAPTER 49

Bobbie called Collette and Jackie and told them her moms address. They both knew where it was and said they would meet her there in half an hour. Cool thought Bobbie, finally someone who believes her. She took her own camera today.

Bobbie got there first and was looking around outside for anything that could possibly show that someone was there. It hadn't rained or anything, so there were no muddy footprints. Dang it! She thought, they always have footprints on television! Moms flowers hadn't been disturbed either. Other than the door not being closed all the way there wasn't any evidence in that room. She waited for her friends on the enclosed porch. She missed her mom having a cup of tea out here. She could almost feel her spirit.

Collette and Jackie finally got there, thank goodness, she was about to tear up again. "Hey guys" she said to them as they walked in the patio. "Remember I told you about my mom's friends and how everything came back as allergy, and accident, and heart attack. I got my mom's autopsy papers and they said heart attack too. But check this out; the coroner said she had high sodium levels. She doesn't use sodium. She uses a salt substitute." Collette said "yeah but there's salt in everything you buy". Bobbie told her "I know, but that would leave a normal amount of sodium in her system. She didn't add salt. When she came to my house for her work supper, I use a salt substitute too!" Jackie said "yeah but you don't know what else she ate when you weren't there." Bobbie told both of them "I don't think she ate a lot of salt though guys. Look at her bike too. You can see where it set for more than a year, now all of a sudden it's over here. You can't even see the television. I know my mom watched wrestling while she rode it. Who exercises in their living room, when you can't see the television?" They both agreed with that statement. Then she took pictures with her camera of where the bike was and the marks on the floor where it belonged. Bobbie took both of them in the sliding door room too and showed them how it was when her and her sisters saw it. She positioned the door the way it was that day and took a picture of it too. Collette and Jackie weren't so sure about the door thing. They went to the dining room and sat at the table. When Jackie sat down and put her arms on the table it was sticky and she asked Bobbie, "what did your mom have on the table here?" Bobbie said "I don't know, what does it look like?" Jackie answered "I don't know, it kind of looks like a piece of meat was sitting here. It looks like dried meat blood ya know what I mean?" Bobbie thought for a minute and said "ooh holy crap, you guys! My mom always had dog bones in her pockets for our dog grunt. She told me they fell out of her pocket at work and Marge and Joan were helping her pick them up from the floor. Her boss, who I think is the killer saw them and said something, I don't remember what though. That was a couple weeks ago, before Marge died even. That son of a bitch must've thought she had a dog!" Collette and Jackie's eyes both lit up. "Oh my freaking God" they both said together. Jackie said "that would explain the meat on the table. He didn't need it so he set it down right here." Collette said "that's the only explanation for that. Nobody puts unwrapped meat on a table, especially when you have so much counter space in the kitchen!" Bobbie said "and guess what else! Her boss is injured too! I talked to mom's friend Joan and she said she thinks he has a broken rib or maybe two. He didn't go to the doctor either. He even still takes the stairs because he thinks no one knows!" Collette said "why wouldn't he go to the doctor or the hospital? That's crazy, you can get pain medicine!" Jackie said "because he's trying to hide something!" Bobbie said "I know! How can we prove it though? He's good at this, but my crime shows tell me, murderers always make a mistake! We just have to find it!" Jackie said "I don't think this guy made any mistakes, he's got to be pretty smug about it by now. He's gotta want to brag to someone. You know how men are, anytime they have something to brag about, they do! Look at our evidence though you guys. The autopsy said heart attack for your mom. Her friend's autopsies came back as common things too. The police will think we're crazy! They won't even look into it. We have a bike that was moved and a sliding door ajar, and meat stains on the table." Collette said "yeah that's true; we don't have anything the police would see as a crime. They'll think maybe your mom moved the bike to clean under it or something and just didn't put it back yet, or the EMTs moved it when they were here. The door, who knows, a lot of older people don't close them all the way. The meat stain, I don't even know what to think about that. They might think she got it out for your dog. I believe you, but I don't know what we can do about it." Bobbie said "plus we have my mom called me who's ten minutes away instead of Val who's a block away! Mom knew I was serious when I told her I thought someone was killing them. I think she called me to tell me I was right, but she couldn't because she was dying when I was on the phone with her! Dang it! If that bastard gets away with this I'm gonna be super pissed! I'm super pissed anyway! If he bragged to anyone I would think it would be his Vice President, Bill, they've been friends a long time. If he bragged, I don't know he might just be keeping it all inside. If that's the case, he's going to crack! I hope it's soon too. I'm going to get my pictures developed at the one hour photo at work tomorrow, and then I'm going to the police station to see if they believe me. Cross your fingers ladies." Collette and Jackie were getting mad too. They both told Bobbie good luck and to keep them informed! The evidence all pointed to murder but this guy was crafty! How could they catch him?

# CHAPTER 50

Bobbie was reluctantly back to work. She didn't think she was ready to go back, but you have to pay the bills. It was a rough first day. Everyone who didn't make it to the funeral was telling her they were sorry. It really just wanted to make her tear up and cry. She understood people felt they had to tell her that though and once she saw everyone, it would get better. Even her regular customers would tell her they were sorry about her mom, and give her a hug. She made sure she always had a tissue for when she would tear up from all the sympathy. Everyone at the store knew mom too. She came in and shopped there all the time. While she was there Bobbie had her pictures developed. To just look at them, you wouldn't see anything out of the ordinary. She was hoping to talk to a detective after work today. They needed to understand that something was going on at Coble communications! She wasn't going to mention any names though. They're the detectives; they knew how to do their jobs. She might suggest Lenny to them, but she couldn't come right out and accuse him. Just because he creeped her out, didn't mean he was a killer. She thought it was him though and wasn't finished with her own investigation. Bobbie told her sisters that she would clean mom's locker out at work. While she was there, she was hoping to run into Bill, the Vice President. Hopefully he wasn't involved with this or she could be at risk. For a minute she thought, maybe I shouldn't talk to him. Holy crap what if he is involved? He and Lenny have been friends a long time. She decided to loosely mention it to him. He might freak out or maybe he knew something, who knows. She was going to find out. Whatever reaction he gave her might tell her something. She didn't quite know what she would do with anything he would tell her.

Finally four o'clock, time to leave. Bobbie asked Collette and Jackie if they wanted to go with her to the police department. They both had things they had to get done after work. Bobbie told them, "that's okay they probably won't believe me anyway."

When she went inside at the police station, they have a big, wooden desk. She stopped at it and asked to speak to a detective. The desk sergeant told her she would have to wait because they were all busy at the moment. Bobbie decided she would wait for half an hour, if they didn't call her back by then, she had other things to do at home too. They weren't the only busy people! She read a magazine while she waited for them. Finally after twenty five minutes, she was gathering her things to leave, the desk sergeant called her name and a detective Bond said he was ready for her. She chuckled to herself thinking, I swear if his first name is James, I'm going to lose it! His first name was Tim. Ha! Good thing she thought to herself. He walked her to him and his partner, Sam's desks. Then he asked her "what's the problem, why did she come down here?" Bobbie started by telling him about all the women in her moms office who died recently, including her mom. Then she told him that "I think someone killed them." He asked "what makes you think that?" She said "I just have a feeling. Plus I have pictures from my mom's house. Her stationary bike was moved and the sliding door was left partly open." Detective Bond asked "have you received the death certificate and autopsy results yet?" Bobbie answered him "yes, I have them for my mom but not any of the others." He took a look at them and said "it says here myocardial infarction. She had a heart attack?" "Yes, that's what it says, but I think someone or something caused her to have a heart attack." At this the detective stood up and said "ma'am, I'm sorry about your mother, and I'm sure it's easier to believe someone did something to her rather than just having a heart attack, but so far it just looks like an unfortunate act of God. We'll look into the other deaths though and see if there isn't something to go on, but right now it was a heart attack. Please write the other women's names on this piece of paper." Bobbie said as she was writing Mary, and Janice, and Marge's names, "but you don't understand, I think they were all murdered!" Detective Bond told her "ok, ok we will look into it. I'll have to see their autopsy results too. I'll call you in a few days, ok ma'am?" Bobbie told him "thanks" and left his office. She didn't think he was going to do anything though. If he went by the autopsies and death certificates, he would think they just died from natural cause's type of stuff. After she left, detective Bond thought she was a sad daughter who wanted someone to suffer for her mom's death besides herself. There wasn't much to do an investigation on. He would look at the other women's autopsies and get back with her though. It didn't look promising he thought sadly.

She went on home and made supper for Tj and the kids. It was strange not having mom stop by for a plate of supper. Even grunt missed her; he would sit at the front door waiting for her to pull up out front. She never did, but he waited there just in case, every day around three o'clock. It was sad; Bobbie got the bag of peanut butter bones from her mom's house for him. It wasn't the same though and grunt knew it. He missed his grandma.

Lenny heard about Roselle's autopsy report and was not surprised. He had been through this before and knew it would come back with a determination of heart attack. His mind kept going back to Roselle saying "Bobbie was right!" He knew that was her daughter and he was concerned about what she would do. He thought he was hiding his injury pretty well. No one suspected anything! If Bobbie was the one who cleaned Roselle's locker out, he was going to be the nicest killer she ever met! He would be so nice, she would have to think, he couldn't kill anyone. She was wrong, but only he knew that he was a killer and that's the way he was going to keep it. He wanted to be finished killing, but decided he might have to kill once more! He wasn't going to let her ruin everything he'd already gotten away with!

# CHAPTER 51

Bobbie told Tj about talking to the police. He asked her "do you think they'll do anything?" She answered "I don't know. I gave them copies of the pictures. My evidence isn't real strong though. I doubt it. What can they do? All the death certificates make sense. Mary with all her allergies and Janice falling down the staircase, and Marge having a heart attack. They were all older women with issues. I just don't think they have a lot to go on. You can't charge someone with murder on a daughter's hunch. Maybe mom really did just have a heart attack. I don't know anymore, what if it is all in my head?" Tj knew she was right about that but hated to see her so disappointed. He knew she felt real strong about her mom being murdered but the police had to go on evidence. They both decided there wasn't much they could do till the detective called her back. In the meantime, they would just wait.

Bill went in Lenny's office to talk about Roselle. He knew she had a heart attack like Marge, but wasn't sure if Lenny had something to do with their deaths. He asked Lenny how his ribs were feeling. Lenny told him "they hurt like a son of a bitch!" Bill asked "well did you go to the freaking doctor and at least get some pain pills?" Lenny told him "no I haven't, I'll be fine." Then Bill went in for the kill and asked Lenny if he had anything to do with Roselle's death. Lenny pretended he was surprised Bill would even think that and said "hell no, she had a heart attack. I can do a lot of things but I can't make someone have a heart attack! What kind of person do you think I am?" Bill said "the kind of person who embezzled from the pension fund and knew you needed to pay it back!" Lenny lied and told him he took it out of their savings. "I used one of our stock funds so Cindy wouldn't notice any money missing." Bill was flabbergasted "seriously? I'm so glad to hear that. That's what he wanted to hear! Well I better get back to work." After he left Lenny thought, holy shit I lie to my best friend, and kill people. I am the worst person I know! He didn't think he was a serial killer though. He was killing out of necessity not for fun. He did enjoy it though, does that make me a serial killer he wondered. He didn't enjoy the killing as much as he enjoyed figuring out ways to kill without being caught. Oh, his adrenalin would get pumping right before a kill and for the next few days he would relive it in his mind. That's just part of killing people... Isn't it? So far he had a perfect record. That really was the fun part to him. He wasn't sure how he was going to kill Bobbie. She was young and strong, like her mother. Roselle surprised the shit out of him. She was so damn strong! The others had been so easy. He hated that she woke up, why couldn't she have just stayed asleep! That would've made it so much easier. He could have just injected her and she wouldn't have had to fight him off. She knew he killed all of them. Right now she couldn't do anything about it. Hell she couldn't do anything about it then either! She knew she was doomed as soon as she saw the syringe. He was just glad he didn't leave any marks on her. She left her mark on him though. He didn't know how long it would take for his ribs to heal! He wouldn't have these broken ribs if she would have just stayed asleep! He hated that she looked right into his eyes, like she could see his soul rotting right in front of her. He felt like his soul WAS rotting. How else could he explain all the pain he caused to his workers and to his victims' families? Cindy still didn't have a clue and Bill wondered about the deaths. Lenny thought he handled Bill really well. He could tell by Bills eyes that he believed him. That was a good thing. He needed to make sure if Bobbie cleaned Roselle's locker out that she didn't talk to Bill. He didn't want him getting any ideas and she would probably have some questions. He wasn't sure if Bill would talk to her about stuff or if he would tell him what she said. He knew Bill wanted to believe that Lenny had nothing to do with any of the deaths. Pretty girls could persuade Bill though. Holy crap! He didn't want to have to kill Bill too! He was stronger than Lenny, he wasn't sure he could do it. He wasn't sure if he wanted to do it.

Bobbie asked Tj if he wanted to go with her tomorrow and help clean out mom's locker. He asked "do you need me to help?" She told him "no I just thought you might want to go. I can definitely go by myself. I actually want to go around three fifteen because Joan will be getting there soon. I want to see if I can get a reaction out of Bill. I'm not sure I even want to see mom's creepy boss though." Tj told her "I'll still be on my way home from work at three fifteen. Promise me you'll be careful! You already don't trust her boss, don't be alone with him!" Bobbie exclaimed "I don't plan on it! I'm not going to let him freak me out though! If he did kill mom he's going to be super nice so I'll think I'm nuts for even thinking he could kill someone. I'm going to let him be nice, hell I might even be nice too. I don't trust him as far as I can see him! I don't think he'll try anything at work. There are too many witnesses. I do want to talk to Bill though!"

When Bobbie went to sleep that night, she had a dream. In her dream her mom was there, trying to tell her something but she couldn't understand what she was trying to say. It was kind of like the phone call the night mom died. She couldn't understand her then either. Why did everything have to be so confusing she wondered? I wish, if mom was murdered it would be an open and shut case! She vowed to herself to find out the truth and deal with it no matter what she had to do! She just hoped she wouldn't have to die to prove it.

# CHAPTER 52

Collette, Jackie and Bobbie all worked days the next day. They asked her how it went at the police station. Bobbie told them "I don't think they're going to do anything. He told me he needed to check into the other ladies autopsies. We all know he's not going to find out anything new doing that. I'm not going to hold my breath for any help from them. He came right out and said my mom died from a heart attack. He thinks I just want someone else to suffer since I am. The detective was kind of a jerk! I'm going to keep going with my own investigating. You guys can help if you want. Today's the day I'm going up to moms work and cleaning out her locker and while I'm there I'm going to talk to the Vice President of the company. What kind of reaction do you guys think I'll get out of him? He's known Lenny the longest. If anyone knows something suspicious, it would be Bill." Jackie said "well if he won't look you in the eyes, you know he's hiding something." Collette said "if he starts fidgeting or rocking his body from side to side, that is a sign he knows more than he's saying too." Bobbie told them "I'm a little apprehensive about seeing Lenny because I just know he's guilty as hell! Collette and

Jackie both at the same time said "don't be anywhere alone with him!" "Trust me, I won't" said Bobbie. She also said "the guard will probably be with me too. I kind of do want to be alone with him, and then maybe I could trick him into saying something!" Jackie said "no, maybe you could just get half of her stuff. Then you'll have to go back, and he might be more comfortable by then." Collette said "yes! He'll think he got away with it and be more relaxed about all of it." Bobbie told them "I'm still going to try and trick him today too. She was smiling her big grin that told her friends she was going to try every time she was ever around him. Bobbie wasn't giving up until she found out the truth. They all decided that Lenny had done such a good job of killing the women. He has got to want to brag! That's how men are. Bobbie knew if he did brag, it would be to Bill. She couldn't wait till three fifteen to head up there. She would get to see Joan today too. That made her smile. She hadn't seen her since the funeral. They talked on the phone but that was it. Joan thinks Lenny killed her friends too. She's the one who told Bobbie that Lenny was injured. She said broken ribs, that made Bobbie wonder if her mom did a wrestling move on him. That would be just like her, because she watched it so much on television. Bobbie knew her mom knew a lot of the moves. It pissed her off when she thought about her mom, all alone trying to fight Lenny off of her. He was a huge guy compared to mom! More than ever, she knows her mom called her to tell her she was right! She would've called Valerie otherwise. It just made too much sense!

Lenny was at work, and except for the pain he was in, he was in a good mood. Too good of a mood! He had all the money put back, which was his goal the whole time. He could only talk about the killings when he was alone though. He hated that! So bad he wanted someone to say, wow! You killed four women without getting caught! Good job! He had kept it to himself so far, but couldn't get it out of his head. He wondered if he could ever forget about any of it. Sometimes he wished the memories would just all go away. He wished he could trust Bill more or even be able to tell Cindy. He knew that would never happen though. She would turn him in and leave him for sure. She had such a pure soul. That's why he loved her though. He couldn't fault her for something now that was one of the reasons he fell in love with her to begin with. He wished he knew some criminals, they would be proud of him! On second thought, if he knew any criminals, he would be in jail. Never mind that thought! He liked being free!

Bill heard through the grapevine that Roselle's daughter was coming in today to clean out all her stuff. He wanted to talk to her, because Roselle was the highest seniority employee they had and he always liked her. He wanted to pay his respects to Bobbie. She was pretty upset at the funeral and he didn't feel as though he had properly expressed how much she meant to the company. You just don't get employees like her every day. She could calm a whole room of people with her smile. She often did, whenever there were changes in office protocol or whatever was going on. She was the one everyone went to for guidance. She made everyone feel better about themselves. The women had even put a single rose in a vase on her desk and they make sure it stays fresh. They all miss her and her smile. She touched so many lives. You never know what a smile can do for so many people.

Bobbie was headed up to her moms work. She was excited and dreading it both at the same time. Excited to see some of mom's friends and dreading running into Lenny. All she could think is, I hope I don't screw this up. I want him to know that I know he killed her. She was hoping to talk to Bill first, without Lenny around them. Then Lenny, and if he didn't come around she knew he was guilty. He was guilty no matter what; nothing was going to change her mind about that! She was sure he would come see her. Joan said he was with everyone else's kids when they came to clean lockers out. She would probably have the guard with her even though he knew her personally. She had been up there a thousand million times before. She drove the small car because of what Jackie said about only taking part of her things. The more she's around Lenny, the more possibility of him screwing up and saying something he shouldn't. She wasn't sure what she could do with that information though. If she told the police, it would be his word against hers. He would deny he ever said anything to her. She could kick him in the balls just thinking about that happening. He's such a pompous jerk! As she pulled into the back parking lot, she said a short prayer. Jesus, help me catch him without killing him myself today, yikes or him killing me!

# CHAPTER 53

She parked the car and started walking towards the building. The guard wasn't there but she knew the code to get in the doors. They haven't changed it in over five years. Since she didn't have the guard with her, she took the steps to the sixth floor. It was a good workout. Her legs were strong because she and Tj worked out together on the weight machines, all the time. It was around three thirty now. Joan should be getting here soon. Bobbie was going to sit and talk with her until she had to report to her desk. Bobbie sat at the "retiree table" and waited for Joan. She knew a lot of the women who worked there too. Like mother like daughter, they both liked to talk. She had women coming up to her and giving condolences. Bobbie hated that, because the more people who came up to her about it, the sadder she got. By the time Joan got there she was just about in the throes of depression again. They talked at the table for a little bit and Lenny came walking through the lunchroom. Bobbie was eyeballing him so much; Joan had to tell her to stop looking at him. What Joan didn't understand was that Bobbie wanted him to know that she knew he killed her mom. That's how she was going to get him to mess up! Joan pointed out how he was walking trying to hold his rib cage without looking like he was holding it. That's a sure sign of hiding something Bobbie thought. If it was a legitimate injury, he would've gone to the doctor or hospital. Ooh he pissed her off, just looking at him! She had to control herself while he was there. Bobbie wanted to confront him in front of everyone in the lunchroom. She knew he would deny any involvement though, so it would be useless! It would be nice if she only had some kind of proof. She wasn't going to let this rat bastard get away with anything though.

Lenny walked through the lunchroom and saw Roselle's daughter Bobbie sitting with Joan and a few other women. She kept staring at him. He kept thinking, she can't prove anything, even if she does know I killed her mom. He wanted to say, Bitch, quit staring at me! Now she's whispering with Joan and watching him. Crap! My ribs are hurting so bad, I need to adjust this wrap I have on. I don't want these women to know I'm in any pain. Damn it, I have to talk to Roselle's daughter, as the boss here. It would look weird to the other women if I don't talk to her. The women knew he had talked to the other women's kids when they came to clean out their moms lockers.

Lenny slowly walked over to the "retiree table" where they both were still sitting. When he got there Joan got up and said she had to go to work. Bobbie asked Lenny if Bill was here today. Lenny lied and said he was out of the office right now. He didn't want to take any chances with her talking to Bill. She knew he was lying because she saw his car in the parking lot! What a fucking jerk, she thought. She wanted to punch him in the stomach so bad! Instead she told him she was there to empty out her mom's locker. She also told him her mom called her the night she died. The look on his face was priceless! "What, she called you" he said. Bobbie answered "yes, she moaned like she fell, if I would have known she was having a heart attack, I would've called an ambulance from my house." Lenny asked her "did she say anything else?" Like he really cared! Bobbie said "yes, but she wasn't at liberty to tell him what else she said." Just to see him squirming in his seat made her day. "I'm going to clean mom's locker now." She told him. Lenny said "I'll go with you." Bobbie told him "that's ok; you don't have to go with me. I know the combination to her locker." Lenny let her go by herself. Thank God, Bobbie didn't think she could stand looking at his lying face any longer. Lenny was thinking thank God too, he had to fix the wrap on his ribs, thanks to her mom. He knew Bobbie didn't like him; she looked like she wanted to punch him. He was glad she didn't because he was already in enough pain.

She went to her mom's locker, carrying one box. She filled that box and walked back through the lunchroom. Lenny was gone but Bill was in there. Imagine that, she thought. Bobbie walked over to him and said "back in the office I see." Bill said "what, I've been here all day." Bobbie told him "Lenny told me you were out of the office." Bill didn't understand why Lenny would lie about that unless he didn't want him to talk to Bobbie. "Hmm that's strange. So how's it going? I was so sorry to hear about your mom having a heart attack. Are you getting your moms estate figured out?" Bobbie said "I'm sorry too. Yes we're working on the estate. I would rather be planning a cruise for mom than be settling her estate though. It's a lot of lawyer mumbo jumbo. She got real quiet and whispered, "Bill, can you keep a secret?" Bill knowing he could keep a lot of secrets and had been lately answered her "yes" she continued with "I think someone killed my mom and maybe Janice and Marge too, maybe even Mary." Bill eyes got real big and he said "what! What makes you think that?" Bobbie told him "just a feeling I have. Don't you think there were a lot of deaths from this office?" Bill said "yes, but all the autopsies didn't say anything about suspicious circumstances or anything. Wow that's kind of freaky." Bobbie said "I know! But I just have a feeling something's not right!" she told Bill that she didn't get all of her moms things and would come back to get the rest. He told her "ok, no problem." She knowingly told him to keep his eyes and ears open.

Bobbie felt pretty good about setting that conversation between Bill and Lenny up. She just wished she could be a fly on the wall the next time Bill went into Lenny's office!

Bill, true to form, went straight to Lenny's office and closed the door. . He said, "hey, I just talked to Roselle's daughter. Why did you lie and say I was out of the office? Lenny said "I'm sorry; I thought you were out of the office." Bill said "my ass! You knew I was here! She told me she thinks someone killed all four of the women who just died." Lenny said "I knew she thought someone killed her mom, but I didn't know about the others." He quickly realized that he shouldn't have said that because it was Roselle who told him that. He didn't think Bill caught it though because he was so pissed about him lying about being in the office. Bill asked Lenny again "did you kill them?" Lenny answered with a lie "I didn't have anything to do with any of their deaths." Bill didn't believe him but acted like he believed him, and walked out of Lenny's office. Bill couldn't believe how Lenny could think he was so naive. Did Lenny think he forgot their conversation at the baseball fields? It was like a light bulb going off in his head, that son of a bitch did kill them! Damn it, he was naive! Not anymore he vowed to himself!

# CHAPTER 54

After Bill left his office, Lenny began to worry. Son of a bitch, what if Roselle did tell her daughter. I wish I had a friend who was a cop. A cop friend I could trust. They could tell him if she could press charges or anything. He started thinking back to all the murders to see if he was sloppy anytime. He took care of everything at his house. He put the antifreeze back in the garage; he did keep a few sodium chloride pills though. He thought he might need another Batch of that. He threw the rest away in the garbage that had already been picked up a long time ago. He used both the syringes Bill brought him from his dad's summer house. Knowing Bobbie, she'll talk to the other women's kids. Janice's son might remember that he did have a light on upstairs. Mary's kids wouldn't know any difference, because they lived out of state and never saw their mom. Marge, hmm, he couldn't think of anywhere he screwed up with that kill either, unless the guard saw him inject her. If the guard did see him, he never said anything. What would he say, hey I saw you touching Marge's ass, what's up with that? No the guard never said anything. He decided the only one who might have any suspicions would be Janice's son. He and Bobbie couldn't do anything about it though. She fell down the steps and broke her neck! They couldn't prove anyone pushed her. He wondered what Roselle said to Bobbie on the phone that night. Did she say Lenny killed all of them or just her? Did she say anything at all or was this just Bobbies imagination running wild? He was going to try and get it out of Bobbie. Bill told him she would be back to finish cleaning out her moms things from her locker. He didn't say when, but Lenny figured it would be sooner rather than later.

Bill had human resources look up Roselle's file. He wanted to know what Bobbie's phone number was. She and her mom were pretty close so he figured she was an emergency contact. He told them he wanted her number to ask if she was single and wanted to go out sometime. They believed him too, lord knows he dated enough women from the office. He was surprised they even asked him why he wanted her number. It's not really any of their business. Bill knew she was very happily married; he met her husband, Tj, at the funeral. He wanted to know why she thought someone killed them. Something had to give her that idea. Bill wasn't sure if he was going to tell Lenny anything he found out either. That son of a bitch hasn't been honest with him! Lenny was getting pretty good at lying right to his face while looking him square in the eye!

Lenny was pretty content with himself; he wasn't going to worry about any of that stuff. He decided they couldn't prove anything and that was that! He was the smart one in this situation!

Bill called Bobbie the next day. He asked her point blank, why do you think someone killed the women who just died from the office? She told him "I'm not sure I can trust you Bill. Lenny is who I think killed them and you're too close to him." Bill couldn't believe his ears, "you think Lenny killed them?" He was thinking, she's smarter than she looks. When she said that, he knew Lenny did kill them! "Why on earth would you think Lenny could do something like murder people?" He wasn't going to tell her about the pension embezzlement. Even if he did, how could she prove it? Lenny had all the money back in the right funds. It would be Bills word against Lenny's and nothing would be done about it. Bill was remembering all the strange hours Lenny had been working lately. When he worked nights before, Lenny would work the whole week nights not switching between days and nights in the same week. Bobbie told him "I just think he's guilty and he creeps me out too. How did he injure himself, and why didn't he go to the doctor?" Bill told her "he told me he fell and he didn't go to the doctor because he didn't think it was that bad of an injury." Bobbie asked "and you believed him?" Bill answered "well yeah I believed him. He's a good faker because I know his ribs are killing him." Bobbie asked him "does he think we're stupid or something? All the women in the office know he did something to injure himself! They can tell by the way he walks." Bill told her "I know, I told him the first day I noticed it, that he needed to go to the doctor. Crap he's even still taking the stairs instead of the elevators!" Bobbie told Bill "I'm not going to tell you my reasons why I believe he killed them. I will tell you to watch your back though. I think he's capable of anything! I don't trust him and if you know anything, you shouldn't trust him either!" Bill replied "thanks, I will watch my back. You should probably watch yours too! If he did kill the women, nothing is going to stop him from killing you either!" They said their goodbyes and hung up the phone from each other.

Bobbie told Tj about everything she heard at her moms work yesterday, while she was there. She told him about the broken ribs and that Bill called her today. She admitted that she probably said too much to him. Bill sounded like he was pissed about the murders too and believed Bobbie more than Lenny. He sounded like he's had enough of his friend's bullshit too! Lenny must think everyone is stupid but him. She was hoping to make Lenny nervous so he would screw up somehow. She knew Bill would talk to Lenny. Bobbie wished she could trust Bill, but right now she didn't trust anyone in the executive offices of her moms work. Tj wasn't happy about her telling Bill everything that she'd told him. Now he thought she was in danger too. He didn't wholeheartedly believe Roselle had been murdered. If she was though, and Bobbie told the killers best friend her suspicions, he was worried about what could possibly happen next. If whoever was killing people came after his wife, he would have to kick some ass!

# CHAPTER 55

Joan told some of her new friends about what Bobbie was saying to her. She had to make new friends because most of hers had died. She thought Lenny had been acting suspicious for the last couple weeks. He was like a kid who did something wrong and didn't want to admit it. He was always looking around like someone was going to stab him in the back any moment. He would try to read peoples lips when they were talking to each other. Probably to see if they were talking about him. Nobody was, well most of them weren't, but he was so paranoid these days. Bobbie had to be right. The ladies in her new circle of friends decided to watch him every second he was around them. You could tell it made him really nervous. He had no reason to be nervous unless he did do something. Something really bad.

Lenny continued to go in the lunchroom and help himself to cookies or cake when someone brought them in. He thought the women were always whispering to each other and watching him. His conscience was always nagging him too. It would tell him that he deserved those broken ribs. Killing people for money he stole was wrong. They were good women who worked their whole lives and were all looking forward to retiring. They'd earned it! He murdered them and stole their deaths too! That should be Gods decision! He just wanted his conscience to shut the hell up! His own head wouldn't let him forget about it. He was done killing except for maybe Bobbie, Roselle's daughter. He had to think of a way to get rid of her. She was the one telling his workers things about him. She was the reason they all stared and whispered about him. He had to shut her up! He knew she worked at a retail store by the mall. She was trouble with a capital T. He couldn't tell her she wasn't welcome in the office. The other women would find out and that would be super suspicious. You would think if she knows I killed her mom, she would be a little scared. She knows I'm capable of murder, what's to stop me from killing her!

I'm going to visit her work; maybe that will shut her up. She'll be so scared; maybe she won't even finish cleaning out her mom's locker. He was starting to believe all the lies he told himself, and thinking there would be no consequence to his actions. He thought he was above the law.

Bobbie talked to Tj about getting a gun for her protection. She was scared of Lenny. He was a wild card and she knew he would eventually come after her. She wanted to be ready for him. He was huge compared to her, just like he was bigger than every one of those women he killed. It pissed her off every time she thought about her mom trying to fight him off of her! Tj suggested that Bobbie call her Uncle Tom. He was her favorite uncle on her mom's side of the family. Her favorite uncle on her dad's side was her uncle Ralph, but he didn't own a gun factory, Uncle Tom did! She agreed with TJ, Uncle Tom would know exactly what she would need. When she called him, he suggested a thirty eight revolver. He said if they took a trip up to his house he would let her practice with one. She told him she had to talk to Tj and see if they had any plans for this weekend and would get back with him. Tj thought it was a great idea. He liked Uncle Tom too. They were close to the same age and got along great, plus he would get to practice shooting too. The weekend finally got here. Tj was happy to get Bobbie out of their neighborhood, even if it was just for the weekend. This Lenny guy was nuts and he wouldn't put It past him to come after his wife. It was a about a five hour drive, so they packed a lunch for the road trip. Liddy wanted to go too. She loved Uncle Tom and he had kids her age. Mike had to work and josh had plans with friends. Tj, Bobbie, and Liddy all loaded the car and were on their way.

Uncle Tom had a huge house, and would be offended if they'd stayed at a hotel. Bobbie wanted to stay at his house anyway. She wanted to talk to him about her suspicions about her mom's death. She told him about the other women in mom's office and about how her mom's bike had been moved and the sliding door. Bobbie told him everything, including what she talked to Bill about. Him and Tj sat and listened to her ramble on for an hour about everything that was going on. "Wow" was all he could say. He asked her "do you think this guy will come after you? I'm not sure I would've talked to his friend. This could get very dangerous!" Tj agreed with Uncle Tom, and told him "that's why we wanted to talk to you. She needs a gun she can carry in her purse. Something relatively lightweight that has enough power to stop the guy! What all do we have to do for that to happen?" Uncle Tom answered "I can give you a gun but you have to register it and take a concealed weapon class and pass it to carry it on you. It's important to register the gun as soon as you get back to your house. You also cannot carry the gun on your person until you take that class too." Bobbie asked "well, how do we get it home then?" Uncle Tom said "I have a lock box for transporting it home. You should be fine. I'll even write a note just in case you get stopped, but try not to get stopped" he said with a smile. They drove home Sunday morning. They didn't get stopped, thank God!

Bobbie took the gun in the lock box to the police department and registered it. They said there weren't any classes for a month so she would have to wait to be able to carry it with her. She thought, well crap, hope I don't need it before then! While she was at the police station she asked to talk to detective Bond. He told her exactly what she expected him to tell her. "I'm sorry, but the autopsies just don't warrant an investigation." Bobbie told him "I'm sorry too, but if something happens to me. You know where to look for my killer!" detective Bond just nodded his head like he was thinking yah,yah, yah. It infuriated Bobbie that they couldn't see what she could see. There was a serial killer on the loose! She wasn't just a sad daughter of a dead mother; she was the sad daughter of a murdered mother!

# CHAPTER 56

Lenny walked into Bobbies work like he owned the place. He was on a mission to scare her into never coming into Coble communications ever again. What he didn't know was that Bobbie was one of the most tenacious people he would ever meet. She wasn't giving up her quest to find out who murdered her mom. She didn't see Lenny come in and neither did Collette or Jackie. He was wearing a five hundred dollar suit, so some of the girls who did see him thought he was one of the store big wigs. Nobody wears a five hundred dollar suit in here. This was a discount store. Customers might wear suits to their jobs but they change into jeans before coming in here, unless they're from the corporate offices. Lenny walked the whole store looking for Bobbie. He wished he knew what department she worked in. He was trying not to draw attention to himself, even though his suit begged for it. All the women were watching him but nobody offered to help him find anything. They were too busy wondering why he was in their store. He wondered if they knew who he was because of the way they all watched him walk around the store. Holy crap just like the women at his office watching and whispering. He hated that! He walked the whole store looking for her and when he couldn't find her he left and went home. He was afraid to ask anyone where Bobbie worked because he didn't want everyone in the store to know who he was. He wanted to intimidate Bobbie; right now she was the bane of his existence. He hoped he could scare her and maybe not have to kill her. That made him a good guy in his mind. He was trying not to have to kill her. She was going to make him have to kill her. In his mind, that made it her fault, not his. As far as he was concerned, none of this was his fault. He felt like the casino started it, the whole thing was their fault! If they just would've let him leave after he won that first jackpot, none of this would've happened!

Bobbie and Jackie and Collette were in the stock room in the back of the store. They worked in the ladies department and Bobbie was the main person in the shoe department. They were looking for their next week advertisement items. They were back there the whole time Lenny was in the store. When the girls finally went back out onto the sales floor, all the other clerks were talking about the guy in the suit. Bobbie and her friends asked if anyone helped him, but their friends just looked at each other dumbfounded because nobody offered to help him. They couldn't explain why either. The clerks did say he was a man who didn't look like he belonged in their store. Bobbie couldn't believe no one even talked to him. If he was a big wig, someone should've talked to him! Where was the store manager? They should've talked to him, at least found out if he was a customer or from the corporate office. None of them even considered it could be Lenny. Bobbie asked why nobody announced a code ten in any department. That was the women's way to tell the other women in the store that there was a good looking guy in the store. Then they could all check him out without the guy knowing. It was secret store code. The men had a code for good looking women too. You have to do something to pass the time while you're working. One of the girls, Tina, said, "it wasn't that he was so good looking as it was that he looked so out of place. He was definitely looking for someone. Nobody walks the whole store and doesn't buy anything unless they were looking for someone. His wife was probably supposed to meet him here, they all decided. Bobbie asked them "do you guys think you would recognize him in jeans?" A couple of the girls said I'd love to see him in jeans. So some of the girls did think he was good looking. Bobbie wished they would've called a code ten because they would've come out of the stockroom for that! "I bet he changes into more appropriate clothes next time he comes in, if there is a next time. If he does come back somebody call a code ten. We want to see him too!" Said Bobbie. Collette and Jackie agreed, they wanted to see him too. None of the three women even suspected it would or could be Lenny.

Lenny saw a lot of good deals in the store and decided he was going to ask Cindy if she ever shopped there. If she asked how he ended up in there he already planned on lying and saying one of the guys told him they had a good clearance sale on grills. He did actually need a new grill. His was getting pretty rusty and old looking. A new one would make the back patio area of their house look nicer too. They had other good deals, maybe he would tell Cindy, and he would do some shopping. She had to have heard of this store. As much as Cindy liked to shop! Regardless of what Cindy thought, Lenny knew he was going back to that store. He did realize that he should change his clothes before going back in there. He still wanted to be intimidating though, so maybe jeans and a sport coat would be better. These women didn't know class when they saw it! They're just basic, common store clerks! He knew he was better than any of them, including the store manager! His conscience told him these so called common clerks hadn't murdered anyone. They were the better people! They didn't steal anyone's pension! There were times Lenny thought about shooting himself in the head just to shut his conscience up. It never stopped telling him how wrong he was to kill those women! He just wanted to scream IT WASNT MY FAULT!!! He truly believed that too. It would do no good though, he just had to ignore the voices in his head, he was starting to get used to it.

# CHAPTER 57

Bobbie and Emily and Valerie met at their mom's house. They had to empty it out and get it ready to sell. As hard as this was they all knew it had to be done. At first they all worked in the same room, cleaning and packing things up. Then they eventually separated and went to different rooms so they could have alone time in moms house. Bobbie went into the kitchen. Valerie stayed in the living room and Emily went into mom's bedroom. Bobbie opened the fridge because she knew that it was definitely going to need purged and cleaned. It had been two weeks since mom died and food was outdated in there. She opened a little plastic container, not knowing what was inside of it. Yikes, she threw it on the counter, it was mom's teeth! That scared the crap out of her to all of a sudden see her moms smile in a plastic box! The smile that had always reassured her in the past was totally freaking her out now! Like a good sister, she quietly picked it up off the counter and put moms teeth back in it and put it back in the refrigerator and went and got Emily and they called Val into the kitchen. Bobbie said "hey Val, grab that purple container in there, we can probably use it for supper."

Val, not thinking and used to doing what Bobbie and Emily told her to, grabbed the container. She was asking "what's in it" as she opened it. Holy crap! She threw it across the kitchen! Screaming at Bobbie and Emily "why did you do that to me? I can't believe you guys did that!" Emily and Bobbie were too busy laughing to even answer her. Valerie looked at both of them, rolled her eyes, and threw the teeth back into the container and went back to the living room and told them guys not to bother her again! When Bobbie and Emily were done laughing they went back to work. Bobbie surprised that she could even laugh at anything, apologized to Val telling her "I'm sorry, it scared me too when I first opened it. I had to scare somebody else." Val accepted her apology and continued working after she told Bobbie that it wasn't as funny as her and Emily thought it was. Valerie wondered to herself, why the two of them didn't scare Emily. Bobbie went back into the kitchen with a big grin on her face. She was thinking, yes it was! It felt good to laugh! This was the first time she laughed without feeling guilty. She almost felt like mom was laughing too. At least her teeth were smiling. Val was always so reserved, she needed that laugh or at the very least smile, as much as Emily and Bobbie.

Emily found an old notebook in mom's room and was going to throw it away. Bobbie grabbed it before she got to the trash and started looking through it. She couldn't believe her mom had an epitaph wrote on one of the pages. She was so glad she didn't let Emily just throw it away. It said ; EACH OF US HAS AN OBLIGATION TO DO SOMETHING GOOD IN THIS LIFE WHETHER ACTIVELY BY PERFORMING GOOD WORKS AND CHARITABLE ACTS OR PASSIVELY BY TOLERATING

OTHER PEOPLES QUIRKS AND ECCENTRIC ACTS. WE HAVE TO BE OUR BROTHERS KEEPER EVEN WHEN WE KNOW HE SHOULD BE KEPT IN A STRAIGHT – JACKET They decided that they were going to be sure and have that etched into moms tombstone. They hadn't even gone shopping for one yet, but they knew this had to be on it. Mom wrote it herself, and Bobbie knew she meant for it to be on her grave. Mom just didn't know it would be used so soon! There was a book of famous epitaphs by mom's bed, so, maybe with all the women at her work dying, she wanted to be ready. After that no piece of paper was thrown in the trash without looking at both sides to make sure mom hadn't left them a note or something. There were so many things in mom's house that needed going through. It really made you wonder how one woman could collect so much stuff! The girls decided they needed to make a plan for getting it all finished. Knick- knacks, appliances, books, furniture, so many things. They decided to talk to the estate lawyer and find out if they could take some stuff that they each wanted and maybe have a yard sale with the rest, if there was anything left. They decided to leave the appliances with the house. Valerie needed a vehicle, so they decided if the lawyers let her she could buy mom's car from the estate, cheap. Emily and Bobbie didn't need it.

The next day, Emily talked to the lawyer and they said Val could have the car at whatever we all decided was a fair price. Valerie was thrilled to have a car she knew was reliable. The saddest part about it was when she went to Bobbie's house in mom's car and parked out front. Grunt was so excited thinking it was his grandma! It broke Bobbie and Tj's hearts when they saw grunt realizing it was Aunt

Val. He went to the door and was wagging his whole butt, he was so excited. He kept looking back at Tj like, if he could talk he would say "I told you grandma would be back" then Val came around the front of the car and his butt stopped moving and he looked at Tj and cocked his head as if to say" where is she? Where's my grandma? Why is Aunt Val driving grandma's car? Even though Val brought bones for him, he wasn't the same. He loved his grandma and you could tell he missed her. Pets grieve as much as people. I never would have believed it until that day.

# CHAPTER 58

Lenny decided he was going back to the store. This time he was getting a cart and doing some shopping too. Cindy would be so surprised when she sees what he buys. He was going to look for Bobbie, but really just wanted to intimidate her by showing her that he knows where she works. That was the first step in killing her.

Out of the corner of her eye, Bobbie saw Lenny come into the store. He was dressed so casual; she almost didn't recognize him... Almost. She ducked into the aisle; her heart was pounding so hard. Then she thought, why the heck am I scared! He's the one who should be scared! She was mad at herself for avoiding him. When she saw him head to the house wares department, she hurried over to the ladies department where Jackie and Collette were working. She ducked into the fitting rooms and asked the operator to call for assistance in the young teen's section. Collette came looking for a customer who needed help. Bobbie pulled her into the fitting rooms and told her Lenny was in the store! Then they heard over the loudspeaker, code ten house wares. They looked at each other and thought are you freaking serious! Lenny is the guy in the suit? The other clerks who were there when Lenny made his first appearance in the store saw Bobbie and Collette in the fitting rooms. They came in too, "did you guys see him?" They asked. Bobbie said "I did see him, jeans, sport jacket, graying hair?" "Yes, that's him! Isn't he cute, for an older guy?" Just then Jackie came into the fitting room area, saying "Bobbie, your moms boss is here, I just saw him in house wares. Since when does he shop at a discount store?" Bobbie answered her "Since he killed so many women. The other girls around them looked at each other with wide open eyes. They all wondered what the hell is going on! Bobbie said. "I bet he's trying to scare me! What a dumb ass! I'm going to walk right up to him and say I know what you did!" Jackie and Collette weren't sure that was such a good idea. They reminded her that he already killed four women including her own mom. Collette said "Let's go for a walk through house wares, and pretend we don't see him." Jackie said "yeah let's see if he follows us or stops and talks to you Bobbie." Not all the employees knew the whole story, just a few close friends and of course Jackie and Collette. Bobbie told them "don't leave me alone with him, we need witnesses!" Collette reminded her "we're not doing anything except walking by him. You can't do anything in the store and neither can he." Jackie said "come on, let's go". The three of them took off on their walk. House wares was actually on the way to the stockroom anyway. There was always something you could bring out of the stockroom.

Lenny could hear them before he saw them. He finally saw them in the main aisle, now he wasn't sure what his next move would be. He couldn't hardly ignore them especially Bobbie. He didn't know her friends but did remember them being at Roselle's funeral. He decided to let them walk on by him. He ducked into the very back of the store. Then he realized, they knew he was there. That's why they walked by him and were so loud while they were doing it. Damn it! He cursed himself. They're going to think he's afraid of them. Damn, damn, damn! How stupid of him! He hurriedly took his items up to the register and checked out of the store. He grabbed a card that was by the register to tell how his visit was in their store. He planned on giving them a bad review because of a certain employee.

Bobbie, Jackie, and Collette couldn't believe he hid from them. What a jerk, they all thought. Bobbie knew he was trying to scare her and at first he did scare her. The more she thought about it though, the more it pissed her off! She decided tomorrow she was going back to his work n harass him like he was her. Bobbie also went to her store manager and told him if she got a bad review in the next couple weeks, it wasn't true. She had witnesses to any behavior she had around Lenny. Collette and Jackie agreed that he would probably give a bad review. The store manager knew what was going on and expected the review. The bad thing about it though was that it would go through the corporate offices first. When they called him about it, at least he would be ready with answers.

Cindy was surprised at all the stuff Lenny bought at the discount store. She hardly ever shopped there because it was so far away from their house. There were other discount stores that were a lot closer to home. This same store even had a location closer to them. She wondered why he went all the way across town, but didn't say anything. She was the main shopper of their house... Maybe he didn't know about the closer location. Either way, she didn't bring it up because he never liked it when she pointed out some of his strange behavior. She noticed that lately he was really acting strange, not like his normal self. She could hear him talking to himself in the garage. Bill hardly ever came around anymore either. She did see his girlfriend, Kathy, at school. Cindy knew they were not exclusive but noticed Kathy talked about Bill more lately. She hoped they got married; they were so good for each other. Sometimes other people see it before the actual couple does. Cindy knew life was too short to not have real love in your life. She hoped for the best for Kathy and Bill. She asked Lenny if Bill was coming over for the football game on Saturday. He told her that he hadn't invited him but that he could invite him tomorrow at work. Lenny didn't really want to be around Bill, he actually didn't want to be around anyone from work. He couldn't tell Cindy that though, so he just played along. After all, isn't that all he was doing lately, playing a role? He knew his life had gone from living a life to going through the motions of living a life. Nobody understood him anymore and he was alone. He couldn't talk to anyone but himself about everything that he'd done lately. Ugh he just wanted it to all be over! He hoped after he was finished with Bobbie, that he could get his real life back. She was making things difficult. She always had people around her. He had yet to catch her by herself. Even when she would come up to his work she had Roselle's friends around her. He had to put an end to this!

# CHAPTER 59

Cindy decided she would invite Kathy and Bill over for Saturday's game. She was tired of Lenny being the only one who could invite people to their house. The next day at school, she invited them over. Kathy, without even calling Bill said "sure, we can come over. Let's cook on the grill" Cindy said "ok how about sausages and a healthy salad, then we can have strawberry pie for dessert". "Sounds good to me" said Kathy. Cindy asked Kathy "are you and Bill exclusive now?" Kathy told her "I'm not sure about exclusive, I'm kind of afraid to bring it up but he's been at my house every night." With a big smile she said "I don't know when he would be with anyone else." That made Cindy happy, she knew Bill wouldn't be there every night and still be seeing other women.

Later that evening Cindy told Lenny that she had invited them over for Saturday. Lenny didn't act surprised or anything, he just said "oh good because I forgot to say anything to Bill." He didn't really forget, he was hoping Cindy would forget. "Well crap" he thought in his head, "now I have to put up with Bill in my home."

Kathy told Bill, they were going to Cindy and Lenny's on Saturday for the game. Bill was fine with going there. In his head he was thinking he might be able to squirm something out of Lenny. Get a few beers in him and he might put his guard down and forget all of the secrets he's been keeping and say something about all of them. Lenny thought before saying anything anymore. He was too cautious with his words and made everyone around him uncomfortable. This might prove to be an eventful evening. At least Bill could hope, he had two days to figure out how he could trick Lenny into saying something about the murders.

The three sisters met at their mom's house again after work. They got busy sorting through things they had long forgotten about. Mom had all of their old report cards and some of the reports they'd done in school. They were all surprised she still had some of this stuff. Even Valerie had been out of school for fifteen years already. Bobbie wasn't that surprised because she had a file for each of her kids with things in it from kindergarten on through whatever grade they were in now. That might be where she got the idea from; she was going to give her kids theirs when they got married though. She wanted to be there when they saw what all she had kept. Stupid things and serious things, just like her mom had for them.

You would be surprised how something as stupid as a bowl you grew up with that was always used for cream cheese and horseradish dip could make you cry. It's the memories associated with the little things you take for granted while growing up that mean the most. Bobbie got the carnival glass bowl her mom had, she loved it because of all the purple it had in it. Her mom loved purple as much as Bobbie. She also got the "red bowl" it was a red glass bowl that was always on the dining room table. Other families would've used it for fruit or candy, but in their house it was a catch all bowl... Keys, change just little things were always thrown in it. Emily got the "dip bowl" and Valerie got the "casserole bowl." It was used at every holiday usually for scalloped corn, a dish their mom made so well. They all loved it. This bowl was tan with an Indian corn trim around the top of it. The "dip bowl" was really just a white baking bowl. Silly, but it really is the little things that turn into the big things when someone you love passes away. It really makes you want to stop and reevaluate all the things you think are important. You start asking yourself questions about some of the decisions you've made in your lifetime. It also makes you wonder, what will your own kids remember about growing up, will they be nostalgic about holidays past or will they just accept everything as it comes? Will they make their own new traditions with families that they marry into? What really is important, it's not really a dip bowl or casserole dish or even the key bowl... It's what surrounded those memories that's important. We, as parents have to make those memories. Being in mom's house brings the memories back threefold. Making cookies on the cookie sheets, eating dinner at the table every night together. Cooking that dinner, or making lunch. Bobbie would never forget Sunday breakfasts either, homemade biscuits and gravy with eggs and bacon. Sunday's mom always listened to country music on the radio. The rest of the week the girls usually had it on the pop music station, but Sunday was mom's day to pick the radio station. Now looking back Bobbie was glad she was exposed to so many different genres of music. Once, when she was suspended from school in seventh grade for writing dumb ass on the chalkboard. She was ordered by the principal and her mom to apologize to the teacher and Bobbie said "I'm sorry you're a dumb ass". She was suspended for three days and mom made her listen to opera music the whole time while she washed the kitchen walls. It was a big kitchen too! She didn't like it then but now had an appreciation for opera music.

They packed some of mom's things and took some of them home. It was a huge task going through fifty seven years worth of stuff, but worth every minute. Emily wanted to dig up some of moms flowers from outside. She felt like she could plant them at her new house and mom would be a part of it. Valerie wanted some of mom's flowers too. She felt the same as Emily, they would have a part of mom in their own yards and she could finish watching the kids grow up. Bobbie didn't mind, her and Tj were planning on moving within the next five years so she didn't want to take flowers now. She could get some starts off of Valerie or Emily later. They planned to meet again at moms on Saturday, the guys could watch the game together and maybe mow moms yard and weed eat it while they worked. They could cook on the grill and have a picnic type of lunch at Valerie's since it was only a block away.

The next day at work Bill approached Lenny to talk about Saturday and the game. "So I guess Kathy and I are coming over Saturday for the game. She said her and Cindy decided we would cook some sausages on the grill." Lenny said "well if Cindy and Kathy arranged it already, I guess you are coming over. I don't want to talk about work though while you're there. I'm getting sick of this place; I think most of these women are crazy!" Bill just looked at him dumbfounded. He answered "ok Lenny, whatever". He was thinking they're crazy; you're the one who's gone completely nuts around here. Still haven't gone to the doctor about your ribs. What kind of fool doesn't go to the doctor for broken ribs? He walked out of Lenny's office while saying "we'll see you Saturday".

# CHAPTER 60

Friday was a bright sunny day. Bobbie figured it was getting into Indian summer and she was fine with that. She decided to make some cabbage rolls for her family for supper and since she was going to Coble communications today, she was going to take some for Joan too. She drove to the store and bought what she needed for the cabbage rolls. When she got home she started mixing her rice and meat while the water started boiling for the cabbage leaves. She set the mixture aside while she cooked the cabbage leaves two at a time. That's how mom always cooked them. When the first two were done she put two more leaves in the water and loosely stuffed the cooked two. It takes longer doing it this way, but Bobbie helped her mom make this so many times. She just wanted to pretend for a moment that mom was right there with her and maybe her spirit was there. We really never know. She made two of those aluminum pans full, poured crushed tomatoes and stewed tomatoes over the top. She knew this was going to be a good batch, they smelled incredible. Sometimes mom cooked them on top of the stove but Bobbie decided to bake them because it was just easier with the kind of pans she used. She covered them with foil and threw them in the oven at 350 degrees. Then she took a break and went and sat on the porch swing for awhile. It was calming to sit on the swing and watch traffic drive by her house. When Tj and her sat on the porch in the evenings after the kids were in bed or doing their own thing, they would play a game of "where are they going". Sometimes you could tell by how people were dressed or if they were laughing. It was nice being married to your best friend. Sometimes they just cuddled on the swing and talked about their day too.

Lenny sat in his office, his ribs were hurting more today than they had before. He was totally dreading having to spend Saturday with Bill and Kathy. He wished Cindy would never have invited them. It put him into a bad mood for the entire day. He hated that because it was Friday, everyone's favorite day of the week. All the women who had the weekend off were in good moods and talking about their plans, blah, blah,blah was all he heard as they talked on and on to him. Just shut up and eat your lunch, he thought.

Cindy loved working with Kathy, they got along so well. It was kind of like having another sister. One she gets to see a lot. How does the saying go: friends are the family you get to pick. Something like that, she thought with a smile. Cindy told Kathy to just bring sausages and buns and her and Lenny would have everything else. She had more time than Kathy to stop at the store. She decided to make the strawberry pie herself rather than buy a store bought pie. The salad would be easy, plus Kathy could help her cut up veggies for salad. She was looking forward to having them over tomorrow. Lenny had been such a deadbeat lately. He never wanted to do anything, just hang out in the garage talking to himself!

Bill was looking forward to tricking Lenny into saying something...anything about the murders. He planned on getting a case of beer for tomorrow on his way home after work. Ever since he went on vacation to his parent's house in Florida, he appreciated seeing only one woman. He decided this weekend he would ask Kathy to only see him and he would do the same for her. This was a big step for Bill. He was used to dating three women at a time, but decided he was getting too old for that kind of thing and really just wanted to settle down with one woman. Kathy was his favorite; she was so down to earth, like his mom. They had been going out for awhile now and he knew she liked him a lot too.

Bobbie turned the oven off and put some of the cabbage rolls into a smaller aluminum pan for Joan. The rest she left in the pan covered. Both pans were in the warm oven for when her family got home later. Joan didn't need a whole big pan; it was just her and her husband at home nowadays. She covered it with foil and went and got dressed to go to Coble Communications. Bobbie put on a summer dress, grabbed a couple empty boxes and the cabbage rolls for Joan. She loaded everything into her car and started to drive over there. As she pulled out in to the alley behind their house, Tj was coming in from the other way. She stopped and pulled back into their drive. He pulled in and they talked for a minute out by the cars. Bobbie said "hey babe, there's cabbage rolls in the oven. I'm going up to moms work and get more of her things plus I'm taking some of the cabbage rolls for Joan and her husband." Tj answered "ok, I'm gonna take a shower and maybe get a little nap in before you get back and the kids get home." Bobbie told him "that's cool, I'll only be gone a couple hours. If you get hungry, you can eat, don't wait for me." Tj told her with a big smile "I'm going to try and wait for you and the kids but you're right, you never know. I might have a little bit then take my nap." "ok babe, love you" answered Bobbie. Tj yelled "be careful of that asshole" as she was backing out of the drive. Bobbie just looked at him and smiled, she was thinking, that asshole better watch out for me!

# CHAPTER 61

It was such a beautiful day, Bobbie decided to drive through the zoo parking lot on her way there. Her mind was filled with so much anger towards her mom's boss. He had some nerve! Going to her funeral and acting so concerned. She knew from her crime shows, the murderer always goes to the funeral of their kills. This jerk went to every one of the funerals! Ugh, the more she thought about it the more it pissed her off. Why didn't mom believe her when she told her it was murder? Joan believed her the minute she told her. That could be because mom was gone now too. Joan's new friends believed it too. Sometimes we're just so naive and trusting about people! Not any more Bobbie vowed to herself!

Joan got to work and was sitting at her regular table. She had thrown the little cardboard nameplate that said "retiree table" away after Roselle passed away. It was almost like the plaque was a curse. She truly missed her friend, all the women did. They all missed her infectious smile. There were some women who tried to take her place. They didn't have the heart or the smile and it wasn't the same. They could take her place in leadership things but nothing else. Joan was retiring in a couple years and didn't have the heart to even try to take Roselle's place. Bobbie called her this morning and said she was coming up to work tonight. She was looking forward to seeing her.

Bill knocked on the door to Lenny's office. Why does he always close his door lately, he wondered. Bill knew Lenny had secrets, but to tell you the truth, he wasn't sure if he wanted to know those secrets. Part of him knew Lenny was involved with some of the women's deaths around work. Even knowing that, he still craved some normalcy between him and Lenny. He heard Lenny say "come on in" and entered the office. As he walked through the door, Lenny looked up and saw it was him and motioned for him to sit down. As Bill sat he took a deep look at his old friend. He looked old today. He thought, that's what secrets do... They steal your youth. Regardless of your age and stature, secrets are like worries, they take today from you. He wasn't sure why he knocked on Lenny's door so he started talking about football.

Lenny thought everyone was phony around him now. His wife, his so called friends, the people in the executive offices, and especially the women in his workforce. He knew he had caused it all too, but refused to take the blame. All the whispers and the pointing by everyone. He knew he was paranoid all the time. What he didn't realize was that everyone else saw it too. I guess paranoia breeds more paranoia. Now he had Bill in his office rambling on about football. Lenny wondered what does he want from me? Things will never be the same between us. We can sit here and talk about football or the weather or whatever all day but it won't bring back the friendship we had before. His conscience told him..That's right, it will never be like before you killed those women, you caused this! SHUT UP he thought to himself. What he really wanted to tell Bill was that he was sorry he ever took that money. That's what started everything. He couldn't tell that to Bill though because then Bill would know for a fact that he had killed all of them, except Carol, she really did die In her sleep. Even that thought didn't make him feel any better. Ugh he hated his life now. It wasn't really his life anymore; he'd changed so drastically he didn't even know who he was anymore. Who would've ever thought the little kid who was getting bullied would grow up to be such a conniving monster! Crap! He forgot Bill was talking. His own thoughts took over in his head all the time now. He had to scramble to think of something to say about football.

Lenny and Bill were talking in the office when Lenny looked at his watch. Anything to get Bill to shut up and get out of his office. He was so tired of the charade. Three thirty, wow would you look at the time. "I'm getting out of here early today" he told Bill. "Okay then, I guess we'll see you guys tomorrow" said Bill. Lenny stood and ushered Bill out. After he left he told Janet he was leaving early and closed his door.

Bobbie pulled into the parking lot and sat in the car for a while. She was wondering what she would really do if she ran into Lenny. As much as she knew she would love to kill him, she knew she wasn't that kind of person. She rolled her eyes at herself. He was going to get away with all those murders! How was this fair? She had to let it go because he certainly wasn't worth going to prison for or missing her own kids growing up. She wanted to be there for the weddings and grandchildren she knew she would eventually have. He was turning her into a bitter woman. Right then and there she put it in God's hands. It was too big for her to shoulder anymore. Sometimes life really sucks! She got out of her car, grabbed the boxes and cabbage rolls and started walking towards the building. This was the last time she was going to go into this building and she knew it.

# CHAPTER 62

Bill left Lenny's office also knowing that things would never be the same again between the two of them. The way he wasn't even paying attention to him when he spoke, and rushing him out of his office. What a jerk he thought! He wished Kathy wouldn't have accepted their invite for tomorrow. He felt bad for Cindy because she was stuck with him. Bill wondered if Lenny was as strange at home as he was at work lately. He looked at Janet on his way out of the office and she just shrugged her shoulders. She knew he was acting weird lately too. Bill decided he was going to talk to Kathy about not going to Lenny and Cindy's house anymore. Her and Cindy could still be friends at school or wherever but he was finished with Lenny.

Joan and a couple friends were sitting at their table talking. She kept an eye out for Bobbie, knowing she was coming up today. She usually gets here before work actually starts. They were all talking about canning tomatoes and salsa. Lenny stopped at their table for a short chat. They didn't know why, they all would've been happy if he would have just walked right on by. After he left they all made eye contact and said "asshole" under their breath. That made them all laugh at the same time. The other tables looked over at them and were glad to see this group of older women laughing and smiling about something... Anything. They have been so sad since Roselle died. It made it feel like old times, when people were happier around here.

Bobbie punched the code into the code box. The guard must've been in the bathroom or busy doing something else. He was nowhere to be seen. She was used to that though and didn't think anything about it. Even though she had two boxes and a square tin pan of cabbage rolls, she decided to take the stairs. The challenge would be good for her.

Lenny walked through the lunchroom on his way out. He stopped at Joan's table and chit chatted for a couple minutes. Then he made a beeline for the stairwell. His ribs were killing him and he just wanted to be home where he could at least hold his side and adjust the wrap he had on them. He was always afraid someone would walk in on him when he adjusted it at work. When were they going to get better he wondered. It seemed like they were getting worse and worse. He could hear the table of women he was just talking to loudly laughing about something through the stairwell door. He was so tired of them making fun of him and talking about him behind his back! Nobody was ever on the steps and he truly appreciated that. He could go as slow as he wanted and still get a little exercise in for the day. He stopped at the top of the stairwell to adjust the wrap he had on his ribcage.

Bobbie got to the second floor and could hear someone above her on the steps. She couldn't tell who it was by looking because you couldn't see up or down the steps. She wasn't worried though, she just figured it was one of the younger girls getting their exercise too. Lenny always took the stairs too, but it was too early for him to be leaving work. She kept climbing, one step at a time.

Lenny heard someone in the stairwell and thought, shit! Now I have to walk right and let go of my ribcage. He kept descending the steps one slow step at a time. He was hoping whoever it was would get to their floor before he got down that far. He just wasn't in the mood for any more people today!

They both got to the fourth floor at the same time. Lenny saw it was Bobbie and couldn't believe he could get that lucky. They were the only people in the stairwell. He stopped in his tracks right there and got his bearings. He didn't want to get caught off balance. Holy shit, he knew his ribs were killing him because of her mother! If he could get rid of her today, his life would be back to normal. He stood up as tall as he could get himself to try and intimidate her.

Bobbie saw it was Lenny on the steps and she thought, holy shit! She hated that she didn't have her gun permit yet. She knew she wasn't the kind of person who could easily kill someone. He had a strange menacing look on his face. It wasn't his spooky smile that scared her; it was the crazy look in his eyes. If he tried something though, she was ready. This wasn't going to end well and she knew it. Would he really try to kill her right here on the steps of his work? She had the advantage because she knew he had broken ribs even though he tried to hide it and tried to look so big and bad. He didn't scare her! She wasn't an old lady, like his prey of choice. She got her answer soon enough!

Lenny, seeing that Bobbie's hands were full and that she was in a dress, made the first move. He lunged towards her!

He was saying... "YOU, you've gotten everyone against me! Everybody always points and whispers around me because of you!" She saw him coming and jumped out of the way. Holding onto her boxes and pan Bobbie told him "not because of me, it's all because of YOU! You stupid bastard, I know you killed every one of those women! You think you're so smart because you didn't get caught!" All the while side stepping his jabs at her. She was using the cardboard boxes as protection. He grabbed the boxes and threw them down the steps. That pissed Bobbie off even more because she just lugged them up four flights of stairs! "Son of a bitch! You think you're going to kill me now too, don't you? I'm not an old lady! You like killing the older women don't you," she taunted. Lenny didn't say a word, he just glared at her. He was trying to figure out the best way to throw her down the steps. He was way bigger than her. He thought to himself, this should be easy! He was having a lot of problems landing a punch though. She was running into the wall as she tried to get away from him.

Bobbie, feeling all kinds of adrenalin emotion going through her now said, "bring it on big guy, give it your best shot!" She wished she would've worn jeans instead of this dress. As she put her pan of cabbage rolls on the landing. "I've been waiting for this day since I figured out you killed my mom!" She punched him in the ribs, "how does that feel? I hope mom broke your ribs! Asshole!" He bent over in pain. Son of a bitch, he was thinking does this whole family watch wrestling? Bobbie said "I want you to admit that you killed them all" Lenny was able to straighten up a little now and said "you know I killed them, why do I have to admit it?" Bobbie couldn't believe he admitted the murders! "You son of a bitch! I fucking knew it! She kicked him in the balls since he was standing upright. You're right, I did get everyone against you", she said with a smile. "Every woman in this place knows you killed those women! They're just waiting for you to screw up, because we all know you're a fuck up!" Lenny was bent over now clutching his ribs and his private parts. He was thinking, get it over with! Kill this bitch! He didn't like being called a fuck up. He told her "I didn't fuck anything up; no one caught me or even suspected anything till you came around! You stupid Bitch!" She was really pissing him off now. He tried to grab her and throw her down the steps. This infuriated Bobbie! "You think you're going to throw me down the steps and say it was an accident." She karate chopped him in his ribs. When he tried to jump away from her he spilled her cabbage rolls all over the landing. "You stupid mother fucker, I worked all day on those! Damn it, now you've really pissed me off! Holy crap cabbage and tomatoes and rice all over the landing. Lenny didn't see it coming, when she went for one last lunge at his ribs he tried to get away and slipped on cabbage and went tumbling down the stairwell. Bobbie couldn't believe it! She stood at the top of the steps in shock.

# CHAPTER 63

Bobbie ran down the steps, part of her hoping the bastard was dead. The other part of her was afraid she would get blamed for his death. She knew he had made the first move but didn't know if anyone would believe her. When she got to the landing, she saw he was just lying there not moving and was almost afraid to check for a pulse. She really did watch too many suspense movies and they always come back to life for one last jab. The good guy still wins but gets hurt in that last burst of energy.

She walked over to him slowly, no movement yet. So she bent down over him and knew he had definitely broken his legs and one arm because they were twisted so bad they had to be broke. She said to him "what do you think of that? You just got your ass kicked by a woman in a dress!" She realized he wasn't going to be able to get up so she checked for a pulse. She felt none and decided we need the police.

She ran up to the sixth floor, and walked in to the lunchroom. She stopped at Joan's table not knowing how bad she looked. When Joan saw her and realized she came from the stairwell and knew Lenny just went down about ten minutes ago. It all clicked. Joan asked "what happened? He tried to kill you too didn't he?" All Bobbie could do is nod her head yes. She said "we need to call the police; he's on the landing to the third floor." Joan said "oh my God! Somebody call nine one one."

Bill walked in to the lunchroom then and took one look at Bobbie and knew immediately what happened. He ran over to her. He asked the same thing Joan did "he tried to kill you didn't he?" Bobbie just nodded her head again. She wasn't sure if she could trust Bill. Bobbie was in shock.

The police arrived and took one look at the stairwell and could tell what happened. They blocked the stairwell off with the familiar yellow tape. Bobbie gave them a statement and told them everything. She even told them she had talked to a detective Bond right after her mom was killed. She said he hadn't believed her. The cops looked at each other like that rung a bell. They remembered the detective telling them about a woman who came in, but who didn't have any real proof.

Bill told them everything he knew. The embezzlement, the thought that Lenny might kill some of the women. He told them he couldn't prove any of it though because after Roselle, Lenny had all the money back in the pension fund. Bill told the police he would have came forward if any of the autopsies had proved anything. The autopsies all came back with heart attacks, allergy, or accident. He couldn't prove Lenny did anything. He told them he had planned on getting Lenny drunk for the game on Saturday and getting him to admit something, anything. They took his statement. After the police talked to Bill, they believed Bobbie. The police asked about a next of kin, the women told them Lenny was married and his wife's name is Cindy. Bill gave them the address. Some of the officers stayed at the office and took statements from the women there about how strange Lenny had been acting lately. They also talked to the staff in the executive offices. Janet told them, Lenny was always talking to himself in the office. She couldn't understand what he was saying through the closed door, just heard his voice and knew he wasn't on the telephone.

The captain and the chaplain went to Cindy's house. They knocked on the door and asked if she was Lenny's wife Cindy. She answered them "yes, what's going on? What's wrong?" She had a sinking feeling in her stomach and her knees were shaking. She let them in her house and walked to the living room. Nobody sat down, she just looked at them. They told her there had been an accident at Lenny's work. He had fallen down a flight of stairs and didn't make it. Cindy fell in their arms In shock. They held her for a minute, and then set her on the sofa. "We have some questions for you ma'am. Has your husband been acting strange lately?" Cindy didn't know what was going on. First they tell her he fell down a flight of stairs, and then they ask if he's been acting strange. "What?" she asked.

"We have reason to believe your husband was involved in four murders and tried to kill a fifth woman." Cindy couldn't believe what they were saying. She was in shock and the police recognized that and asked if there was anyone they could call for her. Cindy's parents and sister lived out of town so she asked them to call Kathy. No one answered.

Bill had already called Kathy, so she knew what happened and rushed over to Cindy's house. The captain and chaplain were happy to see her. It's easier for a friend to console someone rather than two complete strangers. After they left, Cindy told Kathy what they said; the two of them were both in shock. Cindy told her "Lenny had killed Roselle and three other women. She couldn't believe it. Lenny liked Roselle". Kathy said "he must've been desperate if he killed someone he actually liked". She asked "why did he think he needed to kill them?" Cindy told her "I don't know, he's been so strange lately. He's been in the garage so much and talking to himself. I knew something was wrong, but he wouldn't talk about it. I wish he would've let me in on what the real problem was. He didn't even want you guys to come over this weekend." Kathy was surprised to hear that... "Really?" She asked. "I thought Lenny and Bill were best friends. Bill said he's been kind of strange lately too." They both shook their heads in unison and shrugged their shoulders.

# CHAPTER 64

Bobbie called Tj from Bills office. He was eating cabbage rolls and loving that he had a wife who could cook. She told him what happened and he told her to stay there, he was coming to pick her up. A sense of relief fell over her. That made her feel better just knowing he was on his way. Right now, the only place she wanted to be was in his arms. He was so mad that he let her go by herself to that office. She was so damn head strong! Just like her mother! It wouldn't have mattered if he'd told her not to go, she would've just said "I'll be fine, don't worry".

Bobbie called Jackie and Colette too. They couldn't believe it. They both knew Lenny was a big guy especially compared to Bobbie. She told them that "Bill pretty much corroborated her story. The sad part was it was all over money that Lenny stole but could've put back from his own money and wouldn't! Fucking jerk!" They were both proud of Bobbie for getting rid of him.

Cindy called Lenny's parents and told them about the accident. They didn't find out about the murders till they saw it on the news. By then they were at Cindy and Lenny's house.

Both of his parents turned around and looked at Cindy. She didn't know what to say. How do you tell your dead husbands parents that their son was a murderer! She told them she didn't know how to tell them that part. Bill was there too with Kathy. Bill spoke up and said that Lenny hadn't been himself since August. There wasn't anything anyone could do, because he tried talking to Lenny but Lenny wanted nothing to do with what he was saying. Bill told his parents that Lenny came to work the day after Roselle died, with broken ribs. Lenny's dad said, "she must've fought back hard. Roselle had a lot of spunk! I still can't believe he killed her or anyone else for that matter." They all just sat in the living room looking at the television. Nobody said anything but you could see the thoughts in everyone's eyes. How could this happen right under our noses?

Tj got Bobbie home; Collette and Jackie met him at Coble communications and drove her car home. Emily and Valerie met them at their house. Once they were inside, Bobbie could tell them the whole thing, how she kept hitting him in the ribs because she knew they were sore and still broke from killing her mom. They wanted to hear all the details. They kept asking her "weren't you scared" Bobbie told them "hell yes I was scared! He came at me and he's so dang big, and I had my cabbage rolls in one hand and boxes in the other. She showed them all her bruises from him trying to grab hold of her. He tried to push me down the steps! I know he would have said it was an accident. He took my boxes away from me and threw them down the steps! I was using them to block his punches at me. Bastard! It makes me mad all over again, just thinking about it."

Cindy had to arrange for a funeral for Lenny. She decided

to cremate him and have a private ceremony. None of the people from his office wanted to go anyway, after knowing he killed the women from his work. Cindy didn't even want to show her face in the office, she was so ashamed of Lenny and what he'd done. She asked Bill if he would clean Lenny's things out of his office for her. Cindy did call Bobbie and apologize about her mom. She didn't know what else to say because she really liked Roselle too. Bobbie knew Cindy liked Roselle and told her that she tried to tell her mom that someone was killing all of her friends, but she wouldn't listen. Cindy just kept apologizing; mostly she was mad that she didn't see the signs of him going crazy. They all were mad about that though. No one saw this coming except Bobbie and no one would listen to her.

Lenny's dad held a mandatory company meeting. He wanted the executives and the workers attending it. He apologized to all of them. He also made an announcement that he was not going to close the office. He named Bill the new chief executive officer.

The police ruled it as self defense for Bobbie and the prosecutor agreed with them. No charges were filed. Bobbie thought you bet your ass! She felt if they would have filed charges against Lenny when she talked to them before, none of this would've even happened! He would be in prison and she wouldn't be bruised all over. She thought about something her mom always said, "What comes around goes around, don't mess with karma! She knows where everyone is. Doesn't matter if you're rich or poor, fat or thin, tall or short, she'll find you!" She looked up to the sky knowing her mom was looking down and said aloud "you were right about karma mom... She found him! Karma's a bitch and so am I!